ADVOCATE

OF

THE ISLE

ADVOCATE

OF

THE ISLE

BY

LOYS MASSON

TRANSLATED FROM THE FRENCH BY *Antonia White*

New York: Alfred A. Knopf

1 9 6 3

L. C. catalog card number: 63-9148

THIS IS A BORZOI BOOK

PUBLISHED BY ALFRED A. KNOPF, INC.

FIRST AMERICAN EDITION

Originally published in French as *Le Notaire des Noirs.* © 1961 by Robert Laffont. Published in England as *The Whale's Tooth* by Chatto & Windus Ltd.

ADVOCATE

OF

THE ISLE

I

I once aspired to be a political agitator. I dreamed of trials and imprisonments—means of proving my loyalty to the memory of a child. As it is, I am only the black folk's lawyer, on this island where they are still called the race of Cain. Oh, I do not suffer from persecution! People do not even point me out derisively. They merely mutter sometimes when I pass: "That's the blacks' official lawyer." They mutter it with a touch of commiseration and perhaps with secret anger, exactly as they might say: "Look at that unlucky chap, what a nuisance he must find his club foot!" I have become so content with my inglorious destiny that the phrase arouses a certain pride in me. I dedicate it to the child. It is the wreath I lay on his tomb.

He came to us one morning in January 1928. My uncle, Emile Galantie—whose young clerk I was at that time—had gone to fetch him from the station in one of those tall upright carts that look like rectangular boxes, with a slit of window in the back; carts you never see nowadays, even stowed away in sheds.

I am trying to put my thoughts in order. That was how it was. Yes, I am almost sure, a blue cart with a black canopy. But suddenly that metallic song of the bulbuls is flooding the world again as it did that morning; too precise for my groping memory. That turpentine smell of mango trees ready to be threshed. Or that coral reef a little to the left of the breakwater, which flashes out, very white, when the mud shifts . . . Ever since I bought back this house four months ago, I have been perpetually oscillating between my memories and my awareness of their futility. I rediscover everything and, at the same time, everything eludes me.

. . . The cart stopped. Yacoob, the one-eyed coachman. Here is André. I am to be his tutor in the afternoons, after my work. The State school at Grand-Bourg is not one of those to which one sends white children and my uncle is unwilling to consider the heavy expenses of a boarding school elsewhere. Suddenly I know that I am going to love him as if he were my own child. His extraordinary sadness strikes me like a flash of lightning and ravages me. I know hardly anything about this little cousin whom I had never met before. He belongs to the branch of the family they regard as outcasts. It is January, the height of summer . . .

"If his father had deigned to listen to me," growls Emile Galantie. "If he'd made a different marriage to begin with and if he'd led a different life afterward, things wouldn't have come to this!—To hell with him!"

He fixes the child—and me too—with the glare of his blue eyes, sunk very deep in their narrow, cavernous sockets. Perhaps they seem cruel only because of those parched eyelids that throw much shadow over them? Calmly cruel eyes. Enigmatic.

"Ah yes," he sighs. "If that man had led a different sort of life! An honest life . . . A decent life."

Doesn't he realize that a child is listening to him, that a child of seven takes in everything avidly? No doubt I should not have been any more considerate than he was then. But now that I have patiently studied children between six and eight—studied them with disillusioned concentration and without love—I know better.

"He married that good-for-nothing bitch, that trollop who, of course, ditched him, and he didn't know the meaning of self-control. Look at the fine result! It's too easy to blame it all on bad luck. I've got more than a simple orphan on my hands . . ."

My Aunt Marthe had not accompanied him to the station. Husband and wife are never seen together anywhere in public, nor are known to agree on any subject whatsoever. The enmity is an old one; I am told it dates back twenty years. Anyway it is manifested all the time in my presence. Week-long silences are frequent and worse than brawling: death staring at death from two sepulchers.

Marthe Galantie's Flemish origin is betrayed in a certain heaviness of the jowls which age has exaggerated. Her rages are rare but, like herself, massive; then suddenly everything collapses into limp discouragement, and there is silence once more . . . She has come to welcome her charge at the gate.

"You mean to say he traveled alone?" she exclaims to her husband. "I might have betted he would! You have about as much fatherly feeling as a jailer . . ."

"Rouget did me the favor of escorting him."

She pulls up her shawl over her plump, heavy shoulders.

"Your charity is always half-hearted. You never put yourself out in doing a kindness. This poor boy arrives at our house like an object—like a parcel! . . . You might have left it to me to go and fetch him from his home since you found it too much bother."

"I thought it preferable that neither of us should be present at the farewell scene. It seemed to me important for the future. Do you understand? Neither of us should be associated in any way with the separation. We are, and we ought to remain, those who have taken him in and given him a fresh start: his new home and family."

His temper has risen slightly. He turns away, then swings round on her fiercely.

"You dare talk of charity—of human warmth? *You!* To begin with, what do you know about children?"

The couple had not had any. The most obvious part of their hatred sprang from that. Each one of them nurses a

6

continual reproach against the other. Perhaps also a twisted sort of pity? Each sees his own humiliation in the other and hates him for being such a perfect mirror of himself.

"Whose fault is it if there has never been a child here?" screams Marthe Galantie. "Answer me that!"

"The fault of your womb," he says rudely.

Once again that sensation, experienced over and over again, that the air about them is troubled, that there is more than the usual oppression in it. André shifts his suitcase from his right hand to his left. He keeps his eyes obstinately lowered. He is making an effort not to cry. Or is it that he has no tears left? The morning is redolent of the mingled smell of seaweed and over-ripe mangoes.

Marthe Galantie tries to take his hand and lead him away. He resists. She does not insist. Doesn't it look as if she had only made the gesture reluctantly? Why? Otherwise what singular, unaccustomed shyness!

"You can't even manage to perform your function of foster-mother properly. And yet you pretended to be the one who wanted to tear him away from his father!" says my uncle.

He laughs, or rather jeers. He gives the boy a discreet shove in the shoulders. The boy cannot quite repress a sob.

"You must be obedient, André. Here, you've got to obey . . . Follow your aunt, she'll show you your room. If you're very good, you'll be happy with us, I promise you, till your Papa comes back . . ."

"You'll be a big boy then, won't you?" he adds.

He was carrying a parcel under his arm. He holds it out to me.

"For him."

"Whatever is it?"

"I'm not quite sure." (He shrugs his shoulders.) "A set of ninepins, if he got what I ordered. Rouget undertook the commission . . ."

The ghosts of Marthe and Emile Galantie dissolve in the morning light. Their two heads have vanished with their secrets. They will never tell me what this child represented to them. Was he the object of an affection that did not know how to express itself—that resolutely hid itself—or did his presence only add fuel to the fire of their mutual hatred that burned under all the stagnation and despair? They dissolve away, leaving only mystery . . . He, my boy, in what light did *he* see them? How many times I have asked myself that question! "Very big": that was all he ever said to me about them.

"What do you mean, very big?"

He did not answer. He was almost frightened. Was he comparing them with his father, a thin, frail man who was a little below average height? Yet I could feel that, when he used it, this adjective did not imply solely a measure of physical size. On his lips, the word sounded vague and heavy. He was speaking of an absolute. So I ask myself a question: whether all those about him, his hosts, as well as

8

Captain Bruckner who frequented the house like one of the family, did not represent an anti-Eden for him, a hell that embodied the absence of his father. To him, these people were big, just as a man about to be sentenced envisages his future jailer as being tall and broad, overwhelming—the prison in the form of a man. And detention seems to him like a kind of god, insensible—and big.

"How about me, André?"

He shook his head. For a moment, his eyes looked straight into mine, very trusting. Then, abruptly, he left me.

I escaped the epithet; I stood apart from his inhuman world because I was only a temporary inmate of this house, like himself. Above all, because I was the only one to whom he talked about his father (later Captain Bruckner supplanted me for a while).

Those were the rare moments when he showed some signs of animation. All at once another little creature. Palpitating. Lighthearted, in spite of that melancholy that never entirely deserted him . . . Undoubtedly it would have been better to send him to a boarding school instead of having him to live with them. He would have had other boys to play and squabble with, and his classwork; other occupations than this incessant contemplation of old people and of the sea. His tension would have relaxed. But my uncle was miserly. Am I being unjust? He had his own peculiar notion of charity, just as my aunt accusingly told him. A rupee was a rupee and not to be spent without much thought and consideration; he did not make two generous

9

gestures when, in his opinion, one was sufficient. He gave only up to a certain point, never beyond it. Bare necessities. Was he afraid of being taken in? Had he been duped too often, as he proclaimed, and had it left a mark on his suspicious character? He provided his great-nephew with food and shelter and that was sufficient.

"You know, my father promised me a bicycle for my eighth birthday, with an acetylene lamp like the one on Jacques Daniélou's. This year, he hasn't enough money. But over there, in Madagascar, I'm sure he's saving up for one in his money-box . . . Do you know my father?"

"Very well."

"Do you love him, too?"

"Yes, very much . . . You're like him."

Still he did not smile. But a look of joy came and went in his eyes. It was like hearing the muffled cry of a king-fisher in the palms by the river on a misty morning.

"Do you like revolutionaries?"

"Why do you ask me that? Do you even know what they are?"

"My father's a revolutionary. Didn't you know?"

"Of course I know! But better not talk about that too much here."

"Why?"

"It's . . . it's not worthwhile. Your uncle's an old-fashioned man. Those things only annoy him . . . It's different with me: I'm your friend."

"It's because my father's a revolutionary that he's had to

10

go away and live in Madagascar. They were trying to put him in prison . . . Yes, they were, he told me so! He's the friend of the black people. He defended them, he wanted them to have money for their children. Do you know about trade-unions? He'll come back and build a beautiful house. Or else he'll buy back ours that's had to be sold . . . That's what I'd like best. He's going to take me with him. You can come with us if you like. I'd like that and so would he . . ."

Fernand Joliet's life had been a fiasco. It was perfectly true that Emile Galantie—and others as well—had seriously warned him at the time of his marriage. He was intelligent, full of potentialities; he would have had no difficulty in making what the family considered a good match. But, perhaps out of bravado, he had married a young girl of loose morals, the one my uncle stigmatized as a trollop, and promptly had a child by her: this child. Would he have lived happily, or at any rate differently, if his home life had been stable?

He had submerged himself in drink. It was a public scandal. He displayed not the slightest decency. He was to be found in the most dismal Chinese taverns where the taste of doctored rum mingles with the musty smell of fried shellfish, soya oil, and rotting refuse. About this time his wife, infatuated with a former lover, obtained a divorce and left him in entire custody of the child. He launched into a tumultuous campaign in favor of trade-unions for the Negro and Hindu day-laborers on the sugar plantations. He conducted it in a haphazard fashion, as he did everything, and they let him do as he pleased, since this agitation did not appear very dangerous to the big property owners whom he denounced with such vehemence. No doubt he was trying to put his own life in order, to forget the terrible depths in which he was foundering.

But it did not make him give up drinking. Quite the contrary. Drinking became a frenzy. He wallowed in the gutter and sank deeper and deeper into debt. Twice Emile Galantie had saved him from his creditors. He even gave him an allowance, partly I think in the hope of curbing his subversive tendencies, and partly so that he could support the old nanny who looked after his son, this André whom no one wanted to inherit. But can a man hurtling down a precipice regain his footing? In October of the preceding year, things had definitely gone wrong. Finding himself with his back to the wall, Fernand Joliet had committed a forgery to procure a little breathing space. It meant prison. After that, his only salvation lay in leaving the country, at any rate for a while, to make it possible for the family to suppress the whole affair. A family of lawyers who had extensive influence . . .

"Do you like revolutionaries?"

"Why yes, my boy, haven't I already told you so?"

(Above us, the banana-bird, so peaceful, was the innocence of the world.)

"It's because my father wants a revolution that they made him go away. But he'll soon come back, I know he will. I expect him any day. Every night, before I go to sleep, I say to myself perhaps he'll be sitting by my bed when I wake up . . . Is it a long way away, Madagascar?"

"Quite a long way, yes. But ships often come from there."

"Big steamers?"

"You'd better ask Captain Bruckner . . . They go fast. Four days, at most five, for the voyage. The blacker their smoke is, the quicker they are . . ."

"I shall be so happy when I see that smoke on the sea! I'm counting the days, you know . . . When I was six, I could already count up to a thousand."

"A thousand!"

"I heard my father say he needed a thousand rupees the next day. It was impossible to find them. So I wanted to learn to count very well. Perhaps God listened to me? We didn't get the thousand rupees, but everything turned out all right."

I am transformed into another person. I am Fernand Joliet. I am that shameful man. How cut to the heart he must be! He wields the knife himself; the wound could not be more cruel. And he cannot find the courage for suicide, though it would have been as soothing as a warm balm.

"André, you've got to be a big, grown-up boy today. We've got to separate. You're seven. Already a man! Haven't I always talked to you as if you were a man? I'm obliged to leave our country, to sell the house, the furniture,

13

the garden that we love. Everything—even the little aca-
cias you planted. I'm a danger to the big white owners,
they won't have any peace till they've managed to drag me
before a magistrate. I am the apostle of liberty and justice
and that's unforgivable . . . So I am going to leave you.
Be brave and patient! When I come back, you'll be bigger
still and we won't think about this business any more, eh?"

He has been drinking heavily. For once he had good
reason. It was to keep himself in countenance. To prevent
himself from going to pieces. But the rum burns his stomach. It has the taste of death in his stomach.

"You'll live with my Uncle Galantie, it's all arranged.
Aunt Marthe and he will look after you, they're very kind.
You remember good old Emile, we used to go to see him
at Grand-Bourg, right on the sea? Always dressed in black
alpaca, with eyes even bluer than the lagoon. You'll often
meet a sea-captain there, Mr. Bruckner. You'll be able
to talk about ships and it'll be almost as if you were coming
with me . . ."

Has he tears in his eyes, Fernand Joliet? Eyes just like
his son's, perpetually looking ahead toward some illusion-
ary paradise. His heart is heavy. He loves this child so
much! That love is his only integrity. Why, one day, did
he discover the merits of rum, the fiery oblivion of rum,
the goading whiplash of rum? He hates alcohol but he
cannot do without it. The more it becomes a fixed habit,
the more painful his awakening every morning. As soon
as he gets up, he starts drinking again. To keep himself

14

on his feet. To exist in the presence of this boy who watches him and who, as he knows, idolizes him.

"We'll bring about the revolution together. That will be marvelous . . . You'll come everywhere with me. I shall tell the colored people: This is my big son . . ."

Must he not save face as a father? Be what he should —present a heroic figure—for that innocent whose vision must not be tarnished?

"My boy will found the trade-unions along with me. We'll fight side by side. We'll be leaders! All the people who are unhappy will love us. You'll think about it all the time I'm away, won't you? Promise me? Every time you see a black man, you'll say to yourself: My Papa's going to come back. Every time you hear the wind blowing from the northwest: Madagascar's over there . . ."

Does he restrain his tears? Does he weep over his degradation? He wants to shout: "I'm a drunkard . . . I stole in order to drink, I'm a beast, it's the prison for beasts I'm threatened with."

I abandon his identity and recover my own. All things considered, he is more praiseworthy than I who have never had a devouring passion. So much more worthy of this child who, like all children, has a poetic frenzy! . . . . I re-enter my own consciousness. Everything there is neutral.

"I know all about your father and what he has done. I'm immensely fond of him . . . While we're waiting for his return, wouldn't you like us to be friends? You shall talk to me about him, I'll write to him . . ."

15

I wrote only once, at the time of André's death. I contented myself with guiding my pupil's laborious letters, from a distance . . . How can I admit today that I could have been so dense at that moment in my life? No doubt there is something I am forgetting, something that is past? The gnawing hatred of Fernand? Yet no, I think not. Once again I see a dead child. A boy whose hands are growing cold in mine. When are you going to rejoin him, old man? When will you break out of your strait jacket of habit? "You will talk to me about your father." Perhaps I was thinking about my work, even as I was talking to him, about making my presence felt in that law office where my uncle pointed me out to all his clients as his successor, and my mind was wandering. "My father this, my father that." In any case, on every occasion, I tried to break away on some pretext or other. I was twenty-eight. It is the age when one is mainly preoccupied with one's senses. I spent too much time with Aline Bruckner . . .

II

Punctually every afternoon, except on Sundays, Captain Bruckner joined us for whist. From time to time, Maître Lartigue, the barrister, and his wife took part in the session. These tournaments lasted for an eternity. They were the only moments when Marthe and Emile Galantie spoke to each other without mutual venom. On certain days they even seemed to be in harmony. It was as if a light glowed under their wrinkles. Marthe looked like a withered autumn apple and my uncle lost that sarcastic grin that froze his debtors and his enemies.

Later on, when André had become "my" son, I felt violently jealous of Captain Bruckner. The child never took his eyes off him. At the beginning of the game, he would stand some distance away, then, little by little, come closer. He needed to touch the ex-sailor and he made me think of those animals who come and rub against you and who suddenly look at you with a brimming gaze if you casually stroke them. Was not Bruckner the link between him and his exiled father? He represented voyages and the sea, the legendary main, that old generous and surly spirit of the ocean who had only to be properly placated to render him propitious. The Captain entered and the marvelous entered with him: the smoke of ports, the comings and goings of white tugs, straight out of pictures, all shining and clean, spelling adventure, telling of hearts separated and re-united, of exiles blissfully returning to their homeland, their luggage pasted with labels every color of the rainbow.

Bruckner would swell with pride. I would see him square his shoulders and throw out his chest a little. His gestures became more ample. In the early days he had usually worn a brown suit. But soon after André's arrival he had an old seaman's jersey furbished up and, from then on, never appeared without it. I ought to have been sorry for him; I knew that he led a joyless life, that his two children born of his first marriage and now married themselves had more or less abandoned him, and that perhaps he was reliving an episode of his youth under cover of amusing a small boy. But he irritated me. He provoked me, in spite of himself. One always wants to be the first to be loved—and even the only one.

"Captain Bruckner, I'm sure you've been to Madagascar

many times, because . . ." Or: "Captain Bruckner, how safe I'd have felt if you'd commanded the ship my father went away on!" And again, proudly: "My father's never been seasick. He'd certainly have been your friend on board."

Bruckner had presented him with an old telescope, a terrestrial globe, and a collection of picture postcards of ships. He preferred these last to all else. Our friend implied that he had sailed on each of these vessels in turn. What a temptation to draw attention to the fact that he was lying! I did not do so. It was necessary for André to bask in this climate of dreams. In some way it kindled his hope: it was like a little foretaste of the approaching return of his absent father.

"Captain Bruckner, you must know which is the best steamer on the Madagascar route. What is it?"

"Definitely the *Ville d'Oran* out of Le Havre."

Captain Bruckner's forehead cleared. He forgot his cards.

"Mixed cargo. Two funnels. Twelve knots . . ."

"Did my father make the voyage on that one?"

"That I can't tell you. But I hope he comes home on board her. He'll have the quickest and most comfortable of passages."

Emile Galantie was becoming irritated. This daily whist was something sacred—these cards falling from one's fingers victorious or vanquished, like so many extensions of yourself. Never, never must anyone interrupt a game

19

or distract the attention of a player. "Be quiet, André! Silence!" I think, too, that he resented, just as I did, his charge's quasi-religious devotion to Bruckner. He would have liked to have commanded first place in his affection. Out of pride perhaps, and also a keen sense of what was due to him in return for anything he gave. The Captain was stealing his place here, in his own house. Was not the child's heart rightfully his in return for being given a home? The trespass was all the more offensive because he would have liked to display his superiority to Marthe in this domain. What better occasion? Marthe humiliated before other people, with no possibility of redress; Marthe who—he had long assured all and sundry, without a flicker of shame—had not had a child because she lacked a maternal instinct. I could read all that in his mind. In his eyes, the sea itself, blue, yet faintly ominous, seemed to be rebelling against this man who carried his insistence on "realism" to the length of wearing a little compass, instead of a watch, attached to a silver chain.

Between two games, or while Marthe Galantie or myself happened to be shuffling the cards, he exclaimed:

"This is the moment of truth, my dear Bruckner. What leaky old cargo-boat did you buy your title of Captain on?"

He laughed. That almost silent laugh which always sounded vindictive, puckered his lips oddly under his long-sparse mustache turned up at the ends like a Tartar's.

"Can one even talk of sailing in connection with you? Just a bit of coastal trade . . . Come on, own up!"

20

"Now, now, Monsieur Galantie . . ." (Captain Bruckner flushed slightly.)

"Well, anyway, do tell us, friend Bruckner, what was the longest of your voyages? I've been meaning to ask you that for a long while . . . I've got an idea it wouldn't be a hard job for a cormorant to fly there from here."

"In the days when I was skipper of the *Saint-Géran*, I . . ."

Bruckner stopped right in the middle of his sentence. Neither did my uncle pursue the conversation. André was watching the two men. At all costs, the magic must not be dispelled. All the same, I was furious at being an accomplice. It stung me to the quick. Am I saying that too hastily. Was it my desire for possession that stung me? I kept silence like Emile Galantie and Bruckner, and like Marthe. To keep up the fiction as long as possible. But at moments I felt capable of any form of malice toward the old sailor. He exasperated me. What joy to put him in his place— that man who had never been to sea except on board a modest cargo-boat plying between our coast and the outlying Oil Islands, those fertile atolls covered with coconut palms! He had no right to make sport of an unhappy child's naïveté. He ought to have realized this from the first and not launched himself on this false path of lies. A jay in peacock's plumage! He was soiling a soul by insinuating himself into it under false pretenses. Whatever he might pretend, he was destroying something, he was distorting a harmony, tainting a perfume.

21

I am writing all this now. Thirty-two years afterward! Ought not my rebellion to have died down by this time? On the contrary, I am still obscurely jealous of Captain Bruckner. I wanted . . . and I still want . . . to turn that candid child's gaze away from him. He is explaining the properties of the compass to André—I can see him again, the needle is glittering too brightly, I would like to wrench that compass away from him. He is conjuring up immense typhoons blazing with St. Elmo's fire, rollers in which a man's very being capsizes, porpoises like processions of tipsy undertaker's mutes, and the cold hell of sharks rising up from the depths and making the keel shudder—I rage inwardly. I am only a diligent clerk in a jacket too tight at the armpits; my uncle does not greatly favor spending money on clothes and it is important not to antagonize him. Adventure is not written in evanescent golden letters on the scroll of my destiny; no aura of legend adorns my brow. Everything about me is redolent of obstinate tranquillity, of an assured, secure future. Is not that so, dear Captain? How can I compete with you? I despise Bruckner so as not to be tempted to envy him. When André is too admiring—most of all when Bruckner puts his hand on his shoulder, paternally—I take pleasure in reminding myself that our friend finds himself in financial straits at the end of each month, that my uncle is the master of his fate as I shall be later on when the practice belongs to me, that his love-life has been shipwrecked and that I am one of the wreckers. I hope to be the last of them and to go on

22

wrecking it for a long time so I can savor my lofty contempt to the full . . .

Aline Bruckner is his second wife. He married her only eight years ago. She has always had a fire in her belly, if rumor is to be believed. Does the Captain know, at this moment when he is recounting his stories of whales and sea cows and phantom ships, that I am the latest of her many lovers? I should like him to know. He suspects, doesn't he? I have no fear of scandal: he would not dare make one. On account of my uncle and of what he owes him.

Aline is thirty-six. She is neither beautiful nor ugly. Heavy—and passionate. She loves in fits and starts; I tell myself that is how animals love and that increases my need of her. From time to time, when we do not profit by Bruckner's absences to borrow his own bed from him, we take a boat to Flamingo Island which looks, from the land, like a watery mirage, a green question mark in the midst of the lagoon. A mile out, or a little less, all the mystery vanishes. It is nothing but sand, bamboos, and scattered briars. But all is as deserted as one could wish. I make love there hurriedly, as if with a prostitute in a tea house, a Chinese brothel where the men who are coming after you wait their turn almost at the door of the bedroom, but I get the sensual pleasure proper to my age. Up to now that has been quite enough. Now it is mixed with the satisfaction of jeering at Bruckner.

"What are you thinking about, darling? You've been so

far away from me lately! . . . You've got a new sweetheart, haven't you? Don't you care for me any more?"

"What's the object of all this probing, my dear Aline?"

"I want the truth . . . I swear I won't be a burden to you."

"You're crazy . . ."

"No! And you don't know how to lie . . ."

"What sweetheart? You make me angry with your suspicions. I never go out, as you very well know. My uncle's a demon for work. I don't get away even for a couple of nights in a year."

"You don't love me any more."

She shook her head. She has black hair that weighs heavy in one's hands, a great garland of perfume.

"I think of no one but you . . ."

"No, no, you're somewhere else. Do you think I don't feel it? And it hurts me."

She is not play-acting. She needs to hold sway over a man's imagination, like all women past their prime. Sensual pleasure is not enough for her. She has experienced too much of it, given too much of it. Now she demands affection, kindness—illusion.

"What's the good of denying it? You're with me and, at the same time, you're far away. If only I knew where you were. Who you were with."

"With nobody except you."

"You can't put me off like that! I don't even count any more."

24

"For goodness' sake, Aline, stop it!"

"But won't you understand—I *love* you. I'd go to the ends of the earth with you if you asked me to. Even if it meant losing everything. Even just for two days of happiness and then being deserted . . . with nothing but emptiness and poverty afterward . . ."

I love her, while forcing myself not to see too clearly into the true nature of this love. Shall I admit to her that I am grateful to her for not loving André, for making it obvious that he means nothing to her? She would not understand and yet it is the truth—one facet of the truth. With her, I am not on my guard, I am young and free, the same man I was two months ago. She is my relaxation. She calms me. I forget this new person who is emerging. He has my face but I do not know him. When I am with Aline, I do not know him. And this is so reassuring!

III

Captain Bruckner's house, like ours, opened onto the sea. The terrace was planted with pomegranates and on it Aline grew geraniums and hydrangeas in decorated earthenware pots which were imported for the natives direct from the Caribbean Islands. During the first months of our liaison, she used to hang her scarf casually over a branch as a signal that Bruckner was not at home and that she was expecting me. How far away it all is! And no doubt it was foolishly romantic! But it moves me, as I remember it . . .

In the center of the terrace stood a narwhal's tusk, embedded in a cement base. The Captain cherished it even more than his villa. The spiral tusk was inclined at a forty-five degree angle toward the open sea—toward the world of adventure. It was the symbol of his maritime destiny. Why did I know that it had been bought here at a private sale of certain pieces the Museum no longer considered worth housing? It would have been so much better not to have known! The tusk is still there; the successive occupants of the villa have never removed it. Do the present tenants find it still conjures up vast mysteries? To me, it signifies only remorse. So many years of sunshine and rain have coated it with a hard patina. It still remains and it still accuses me. For because of it André had his first glimpse of the falsity of the world of marvels, the revelation that opened up the way to all the rest . . .

Whoever was it who had talked to him of a whale's tooth? "Captain Bruckner's Whale's Tooth." My uncle's Hindu cook, Charlézenn, who lived at the bottom of the courtyard with his four children and his wife, Charlézia, who did all our housework? The postman? Yacoob, whom the family regularly hired to drive them in his cart? Did they, perhaps, genuinely believe in it? Anyhow, their tongues had wagged. Was it not Moby Dick here among us? Ruled by the fabulous "Whale's Tooth," the world became a place where miracles could happen. Why should not Fernand Joliet soon return from exile, a rich and happy man? The royal spirit of the sea could do anything, since it had permitted the Captain, our personal friend, to capture and slay Leviathan and to keep one of its teeth as a proof of his prowess. Bruckner was his beloved angel, the infallible interceder, the good magician.

"I'm going to write to my father to ask him if he saw any whales on his voyage."

"Oh, he certainly didn't! There aren't any in our regions. They live much more to the south, in the cold seas. Off the Kerguelens, apparently . . . Would you like me to show you the Kerguelen Islands, also known as the Islands of Desolation, on the map?"

"Captain Bruckner's met lots of whales!"

"Did he tell you that? Really and truly?"

(It was no use my smiling.)

"A whole shoal, one afternoon, off the coast of Tamatave. He was frightened—and usually *he's* not frightened of anything. They were all staring at him with their eyes bigger than cart wheels and they were lashing their tails and it made a noise like two freight trains running into each other . . . That was the day he nearly got killed harpooning their queen. His long-boat was smashed into a thousand pieces, but he had another one launched and he attacked again and again till he killed her. The sea was red with blood . . . He kept that tooth as a souvenir."

"Didn't you know that?" he asked, after a moment.

I averted my gaze. In spite of myself.

"Why?" he asked, a little put out.

How often—heavens, how petty I am!—how often I am on the point of answering him that Bruckner is lying, that my uncle is right to call him a captain of ramshackle cargo-boats. But that would be too grave a risk.

"Will you come with me as far as the station? I've got an urgent letter to send off, this very evening."

"To my father?"

"No, a business letter . . . I'll write to him on Monday, your Papa."

"*I'll* write to him too. You'll help me, won't you? I'll ask him if he saw any whales on his journey."

We walk as far as the station, slowly. Captain Bruckner possesses another advantage over me; the driver of the six o'clock train was his servant, as a young man, and he has promised: "One day we'll have a ride on the engine . . ." That hand in my hand is hot; at moments it trembles. It makes me think of a captive bird. André must be a little feverish. It worries me perpetually that he is always so pale! My uncle ought to make his mind up to get Doctor Malleret to come and see him. The bay is smooth, of a tender, ethereal blue. Everything seems to be rising up to heaven. Never have there been so many birds as there are this year in the breadfruit trees that border the road. All about us they twitter and sing and a thousand voices little by little bear the world skyward.

No doubt my unaccustomed hand is not gentle enough; the captive bird in it flutters wildly.

"I'm very, very fond of Captain Bruckner."

(*Please*, André! I can no longer endure the sound of that name . . . Stop it!)

"He's promised he'll have a boat built, as soon as he can and that he'll take me to Madagascar. Perhaps in July? He knows the sea so well that it'd be easy for him, even on

29

board a tiny ship. I dream about it every night . . . Do you think it's possible, that he'll be able to get that boat?"

"Yes, perhaps . . ."

"How *happy* I am!" (He is radiant.)

Oh, God, give me strength not to blow out that light! I open my hand, but the bird remains in it. Where would it go? Who would take it in? The other birds, the real ones, go on singing of the sun, of heedless joy, of the softness of the last shower.

"Captain Bruckner's an excellent man with a very kind heart . . ."

"Yes," he says (still with that luminous gravity). "When he's there, it's as if we were all on board a big steamer . . ."

"All the same, listen to me . . ."

My tight jacket is stifling me. I would give much not to be this colorless little lawyer in black shoes. Oh God, let this child understand how I love him and make him love me more than anyone else!

"Listen to me, André. The Captain's all that, most certainly, but . . ."

"I'm going to tell you something. When he comes into the room and sits down and looks at me, I know it can't be long before my father comes home . . . I tore a page out of the calendar this morning. Charlézenn reckoned that made seventy-six days he's been gone. He must be beginning to have enough money for his return ticket."

"I'm quite sure he has . . . Monsieur Lartigue who's got

relatives in Tamatave told us he'd found a very good job there."

"Why's he only written to me just once?"

"He can't have had time, especially if he's working hard."

We return from the station by the beach road, under the trees where the wind seems always asleep. A smell of fish and dried grass hovers everywhere. It will grow heavier as darkness comes on. A dense canopy of odor will spread upward to meet the rising moon.

"That's true," says the child thoughtfully. "He's working, so he can't write. He spends all his time working so as to get back to me sooner . . ."

And, after we had gone a few more steps: "What a surprise if one morning he saw me coming ashore with Captain Bruckner! He's not expecting it at all. He'll be so surprised, he'll jump for joy . . . P'raps it's because of that ship he's having built in the Morel shipyards, that Captain Bruckner's away today? He told me the day before yesterday he had to cash a check at the bank to pay his workmen."

"He's lying. I implore you to get that dream out of your head, you'll be too disappointed and miserable later on." I choke back the words that spring to my lips. But could I keep silence much longer? Had I the right to? If Bruckner were with us, I'd stare at him in such a way that he'd feel obliged to retract, to admit that . . . that he'd exaggerated a little, that when all was said and done, et cetera . . . He could say what he liked but he would no longer be this demi-god who was taking my child a little further from me every day.

"We must hurry, it'll soon be dinnertime."

"Do you think Captain Bruckner will look in and see us for a moment this evening?"

"Not this evening, no. He's in town, you told me so just now. He's gone there to draw his pension and he won't come back till the last train, as he always does."

The face has clouded over. Without Bruckner, the world is a prison. Nothing in it shines. No tropic-bird on the bay, no lighthouse taming the ocean. Everything is shuttered and dark.

"Would you do something to please me? Something I'd like very much?"

As if I were no longer in charge and it was he who was taking the lead. Why, of course I'll do anything to please him. No matter what! I dream that I too am a captain. I am thirty years older. I have white hair cropped very short and heavy eyebrows and a network of kindly wrinkles. A smell of tar clings to me, under my loose coat. I undo it, and all the illusory magic of the ocean exhales from it for the delight of a little boy.

"What is it you want? Tell me, quick."

He hesitates. We have stopped still. All this childish confidence gazing up at me. Eyes like the eyes of unfallen Adam, seeking the king of glory in Eden.

"I'd like to touch Captain Bruckner's whale's tooth," he said in a low voice. "I haven't had a chance to yet. I daren't ask him, but, as he's not at home, do you think we might?"

"Ah, so that's it, eh?"

"Yes, please ... To see if it's as sharp as a shark's tooth."

... Like other children, at Christmas, waiting for the sky to burst open and shower down a magical rain of toys.

Aline welcomes us. A little rum and a glass of *flan-gourin* for André? She has just been watering her flowers and the three or four pomegranates that give them some shade in the heat of the day. Her cheap perfume mingles with the smell of the wet earth. There is an urgency in the scent. I regret having brought this child here. I am full of desire. That peculiar hot feeling at the back of the throat you get after a calcium injection. At the same time a sense of triumphant indecency. The idea goes to and fro in my head; I am about to make an assault on primeval innocence, I am recommitting the original sin.

"Hallo! We've come to make a pilgrimage to the 'Whale's Tooth.' "

"I think I guessed as much, when I saw this boy's eyes," said Aline.

She bursts out laughing. I desire her and yet I would like to hit her. Her laugh is the cruelty of morning after dreams.

"My husband harpooned that whale in person, did he tell you?" she asked, still mocking. "All the little niggers of Grand-Bourg know the story and there isn't a greater

33

navigator under the sun than our dear Captain Bruckner . . ."

"Yes, he told me . . ."

"Well, he'll certainly invent some fresh details, if you
ask him nicely. The day after he's drawn his pension money
he's usually very eloquent and his imagination is quite
unbridled."

"No doubt because he's spent his days wandering about
the quays and in the stevedores' offices in search of his
memories," she explains for my benefit. "That way, one
Monday a month he has the illusion of living again—of
being alive."

She adds, very low: *"I'm* only alive when I'm in your
arms. Alas, it's so seldom these days ever since this kid
arrived!"

André stares at her, then at me. This laughter shocks
him. Dumbfounds him. Since we are so near the wonderful "Whale's Tooth," ought not the atmosphere to be
reverent? He senses that Aline is being sarcastic and her
sarcasm is like a needle running into him. Something is
menaced, and soiled: the very light of day. A menacing
crack opens in beauty. (Once again, my fear that he is
feverish, my dread of tuberculosis; I cannot explain why.)

"Aline, please!"

"Yes," she says, "you're right."

She recovers her gravity. André had let go my hand: He
takes it again. By what spell of the evil one were fairies
and "Whale's Teeth" not true any more? He draws a long

breath. My head is swimming. I am so little capable of
guiding a child's mind, of separating reality from illusion
there without disturbing it! So little of a poet, in fact! I
must get the boy away without further delay from this
garden of forbidden dreams. We have no business here,
either of us. I do not want Aline's love when he is with
me. Tomorrow, or the day after, Bruckner will find the
Ariadne's clew that will lead him out of the labyrinth of
his lies. That's his affair! Let him get out of it as discreetly
as possible. I'll put him on his guard: "When you've dazzled this boy's eyes too much with miraculous tales of the
sea and this boat you're building and when all's said and
done, you offer him nothing, what's going to happen, Monsieur Bruckner? You ought to think about that. It's a dangerous game . . ."

Nevertheless, André remains at a distance from the
"Whale's Tooth." He no longer has the least desire to
touch it. He resists when I try to pull him toward it. Make
an end of it! Get away, both of us! A slow, insidious rain
of ashes is falling on everything. The lagoon is a stretch of
water that holds no mystery, the sirens have fled. On the
shore, Ulysses patches up the sandals of adventure in rain.
Captain Nemo is dead. Aline makes some vague movement
toward her pomegranates, brushes my hair with a kiss.
"For God's sake, leave me alone! Not this evening, I tell
you." I could not have been more shocked if she had made
love to me on a grave. Over there, in the distance, a long

lead-colored cloud is like the chosen delegate of childhood at the funeral of Captain Nemo.

"Now it really is dinnertime, André dear. Your aunt will be beginning to look at the clock . . ."

"Oh, you've plenty of time . . ." says Aline. "It's only quarter-to-seven."

Her voice is too fascinating. I imagine myself stroking her breasts, I am burning all over. I should lose something forever if I went away now. Yes, Aline, it is only quarter-to-seven . . .

If Captain Bruckner had returned by the last train as usual, if he had made his monthly purchases and his round of nostalgic visits and not hurried home in that unforeseen way—this narwhal's tusk would not be reproaching me now. It would not have acquired the patina of death. At any rate, it would not be my accuser.

Bruckner joined us. He was not wearing his jersey but the brown flannel suit he always put on for these expeditions to town. He was smiling and calm, though slightly surprised—and alarmed—to find me at his house so late. Immediately, a little color reappeared in André's cheeks. He advanced furtively toward his hero, then stopped. Once again Ulysses was sailing the seas on the track of the golden fleece and the sirens were reborn from a lover's tears, The sun had triumphed over the cloud. It was a radiant evening, carefree and ringing with magical echoes.

"You couldn't have turned up at a better moment, Cap-

tain Bruckner! We were worshipping the 'Whale's Tooth'
... Own up! You're inspired, like the storytellers of old!"

He was on the point of embracing his wife. He let go
of her. Was he disturbed? I had the feeling he was. It
pleased me.

I went on, rather brutally:

"This kid listens to you as if everything you say were
Gospel truth . . ."

"Well, yes," he began, after a little silence, "it's a good
story. André knows it, anyway . . ."

Aline was watching him with a contemptuous pity which
gratified me. She winked at me. Bruckner noticed it and
flushed. Now I was being revenged for the drab uniform
I had to wear! A tidal wave was washing away my stick-
in-the-mud clerk's life . . .

"Come now, Captain Bruckner" (I was almost shouting). "Since you're such a famous sailor, don't you think
it would have been plain honesty to tell this little boy that
you've never seen any whales, any more than I've ever
talked to the Pope? That you've never made a voyage
longer than three or four hundred miles in one go and
have never been further than the Oil Islands."

"It could be," says Bruckner.

He runs his hand over his forehead.

"Yes," he mumbles, "it's possible. I'm wrong and at the
same time I'm right . . . how decide what's the best line
to take? I've been quite frank about it with Monsieur
Galantie, but . . ."

"André," he goes on, after a pause. "Do you mind if I

37

talk to you about all this tomorrow? Tonight I'm very tired. I've had a really harassing day . . ."

He looks at me imploringly. I am perfectly aware of this, yet I stubbornly refuse to collaborate.

"I went to the Morel shipyards to supervise the work on our ship," he says, very ill at ease. "Oh, she's going to be a beautiful craft! All white, and as fast as a Customs motor-launch. We shall have a magnificent voyage. Unfortunately, my carpenters and calkers are behindhand. I really ought to be nagging them all the time, but that's impossible. The shipyards are a long way away and I've got a weak heart, as you know."

He has his eye on me again. Am I going to help him or at least refrain from crushing him utterly? I shake my head.

"Do be honest, my dear Captain Bruckner. It's cruel to deceive this little fellow like that. What ideas are you putting into his head? And what are you going to say afterward? The longer you go on, the harder it's going to be for him when he learns the truth."

"I'm wondering myself if you aren't taking the wrong line," puts in Aline. "It would be better to . . ."

"Leave me alone!" he says defiantly.

He is lost in his flannel suit. He could resist us better if he had his jersey, his compass-mascot, all his appurtenances. Here and now, I tell myself, he has definitely been retired for good and all. The sea is withdrawing from his life. An old, old piece of wreckage rotting under the moon.

"Let's not discuss it any more tonight. Don't you think

38

that would be better? Perhaps you know what is the wisest course, personally I confess I don't . . . I think it would be more sensible for all of us to go and have our dinners and get to bed."

He raises the child's chin. His hands have that little tremor they have now and then at whist when he is Emile Galantie's partner and has been scolded for some tactical error.

"Now, boy, you're very fond of Captain Bruckner, aren't you? *He* truly has a very great affection for you. You remind him of his children when they were quite little boys. They too adored ships and the sea and stories of whales and sharks and cyclones. They really *did* make a voyage, on board the ship I had then. But were they so lucky, after all? It's only the adventures you dream of that don't disappoint you. Four or five disappointments and childhood leaves you, with all its bright visions, and you never recover it. We become little men before our time, we take up our cross and we find them all ready waiting for us—the hammer and nails and the sponge soaked in vinegar . . ."

He turns toward me: "Is that what you wanted?"

His eyes are a little shifty in their setting of deeply scored crow's feet. And in André's eyes, a light has departed like a ship putting out to sea, that light of childhood which has just been alluded to. I can see it slowly moving away, a sail, a puff of white vapor . . . Come back, come back! It enters the fairway, the wind is blowing from the north, it will soon have vanished. I ought to have silenced

39

Captain Bruckner, but now it is too late. Doubtless he was afraid I should destroy his whole legend at one blow? He has taken the initiative—he will concede only just as much as he has to. Will I be satisfied then? At least for tonight? He will sacrifice the "Whale's Tooth."

"As to the facts about this," (he drags the child almost roughly toward the cement pedestal), "I'm going to tell you a secret. My wife and your cousin are in the know, but you'll be the only one besides them to know the truth. Right? . . ." (He pauses a moment to get his breath.) "What a big boy you must be for me to talk to you like this! In the first place, whale don't have teeth but baleen. I'll explain what that is another day. It's the tusk of a narwhal. Secondly, I . . . I bought it."

He adds very hurriedly: "I'll try to find you one. We'll prepare the cement for its pedestal ourselves. They're very rare but I'll do my utmost . . ."

He is like someone who has just vomited. If he were younger and stronger, he would have flung himself on me. But he is this old man with a failing heart who has to go slowly so as to put off his meeting with death as long as possible. He contents himself with shaking his head at me, dubiously. He is judging me without passing sentence on me, and that is the hardest for me to endure. The air is heavy with a vast, brooding cloud of nameless suspense.

André is livid. He too shakes his head—he has adopted all his idol's tics—and comes back to me again. A little drowned boy. All over the world, the birds are losing their

40

feathers, losing everything that is blue and red, green and golden, everything that makes the bright raiment of joy. Ah, God, why do you permit these things? Why have you lighted this fire of jealousy in me? He comes back to me. He takes a century to come back. He is drifting on an ocean of fever. This is the dying boy I shall cradle in vain one night when all the ports will have refused him the aid of their lighthouses and breakwaters.

"Captain Bruckner!"

But no, I have nothing to say . . . Bruckner looks utterly dazed.

"I swear to you, André, I'll get you the finest narwhal's tusk that exists. I'll spend all my savings on it if necessary."

It is barely a whisper. His breathing is short and jerky. I did not know he had asthma.

"There. Now let's go home to dinner . . ."

For me it has remained "Captain Bruckner's Whale's Tooth," over there on the terrace whose pomegranates died long ago, where there are no geraniums any more, where the wind has dispersed all trace of Aline's scent. A lawyer's clerk is walking there with a child. He does not know that the child is going to die and that he himself will become a frigid, lonely old man. He has a jacket too tight across the shoulders which humiliates him and the child is expecting from every single thing a sign that happiness will soon begin to bud again. Bruckner's voice: "Four or five disappointments and childhood leaves you with all its bright visions and is never recovered again."

At every random cast, life scatters the seed of death. The soil of ravaged innocence is so fertile! So atrociously, so abominably fertile!

IV

Never did he speak of his mother. Sometimes he would just mention Mélia, the Kaffir nanny who had looked after him those last months when Fernand Joliet had found himself alone. Nobody questioned him. Even if so many years had not gone by, the house would have retained little echo of his brief stay there. What I hear is the eloquent silence of his ever-restless presence. I follow a glimmering shadow from room to room, all my senses on the alert. The noises of the street do not reach me; I could believe that, as in the old days, no one passes along it once darkness has fallen. In the drawing-room, motionless ghosts are seated round a pack of cards. The joker is turned up. He comes and goes among the players and does not awaken them. A vague but insistent smell of carnations trails behind him. One day I shall cease to stalk my memories; I shall be bleached and dry like the whist players in the drawing-room. Then no one will any longer know he existed. Someone will come along, splendidly unconcerned, and throw open the doors and window to let in fresh air.

Recently, I have been on the point of buying the narwhal's tusk. My neighbors do not care about it in the least; I even suspect them of having kept it only out of laziness. But ever since I have told them I wanted it, they have suddenly set great store on it. They are asking a high price and I am bargaining. "Well, well, if that shrewd old fox, the niggers' lawyer, has taken a fancy to that quaint object that always stinks a bit in hot weather, it must be worth something—it can't be just a whim of the late Captain Bruckner's. Don't let's throw away our chance of making a bundle." I am bargaining inch by inch and I am ashamed of myself. Certainly I can afford to pay and everything associated with my child to me is a relic. But who is ever cast all in one mold? There is one man in me who loves; there is another for whom a sou is a sou and for whom a sou overspent is a proof of deplorable fecklessness. That must be a legacy from Emile Galantie.

The ghost of Captain Bruckner leaves the whist players, hovers mistily, then takes a sharply defined shape. What a long face, all at once! A face in which every detail seems to be exaggerated.

"I knew that Aline was deceiving me with you, and that

44

the favorite place for your lovemaking was Flamingo
Island. I was not so very angry with you, after all! It was
something to be expected under the circumstances. She
was hot-blooded and I was forewarned. Perhaps she only
married me as a matter of convenience? To settle down,
as they say? Or out of charity? . . ."

Why does he talk to me of her? Why tonight? Was not
all that blotted out long ago? Aline is in England; it is
twelve years since I last saw her. But he summons her and
she appears. Because she is still alive, she does not have
the now ageless body of Bruckner and of the others who
are gathered round the circular ebony table. She arrives
burdened with the weight of her actual years. A decrepit
old woman who makes me heave with disgust. Could I
possibly ever have embraced this caricature? Did I really
lie on that body, making passionate love to it? In one flash,
I realize all that separated me from André—my commonplace mind, the constant outrage to his luminous child's
imagination. To him, at that time, Aline and I already
were that monstrous couple. Our presence beside him was
filth flung into a spring of clear water.

Captain Bruckner blinks slightly . . . The night has
spread miles of watered silk over the lagoon. Darkness
envelopes the house. I am isolated from everything that is
not myself and my past.

"No, honestly, I never hated you because of Aline. Now
and then I was a little angry, but admit that was the least
you could expect! When you had just been with her and

she was still warm from you . . . But for the narwhal's tusk,
oh yes, I did hate you. Deeply. I wished you all the ill one
can wish anyone. Death is born in us at our own birth, but
life weaves a protective covering round each and all of us
to avert it as long as possible. For André, the narwhal's
tusk should have remained the fabulous, comforting
'Whale's Tooth.' "

Aline laughs. As she laughed on that evening long ago.
Exposing three quarters of her yellow teeth. All that croco-
dile-skin round her cheekbones . . . The undertaker's mute
whom I loved, who was burying the marvelous and whom
I followed without realizing where I was going. Oh, my
boy!

Bruckner is watching her and watching me. He has an
immaculate jersey, very stiff, that looks as if it had been
starched. His compass glitters dazzlingly at the end of his
silver chain. He does not stir, but his gaze is commanding.
Meekly, Aline comes close to me. Our shoulders touch.

"You were two specters," says Bruckner. "You already
had the faces you have today. In any case, they were already taking shape in you. Your mission was to ravage that
innocent life and you were fulfilling your task."

"No!"

"Admittedly, you were doing it without realizing it;
but you were most certainly doing it and doing it ruth-
lessly. I'm going to tell you two things, and I've no doubt
that you'll pay attention to what I say. The first, obviously,
is that you wanted to humiliate me in André's eyes, to de-

stroy that image of the kind captain he loved—in brief, to make me disappear from his horizon so that his child's soul should be all yours. The second? Well, I don't think I'm telling you anything you don't know already. You needed to lower me as well in the eyes of my wife—of this specter. You possessed nearly all of her but that was not enough for you. It was necessary to you that I should have nothing left . . ."

I tried vainly to disengage myself from the specter. Did we really love each other so much? But I am stuck to her as if we were glued together. Her shoulder caresses mine.

"Aline," demands Bruckner, "wasn't that so? Didn't you feel it?"

"Yes, it was so," replies Aline.

"Ever since that evening on the terrace, I have been expelled from what was probably not love, rather pity or kindly patience—anything you like—but at least it was some sort of warmth. I have felt as if I were naked and I have shivered. To the day of my death, I was cold. Aline's previous infidelities had never condemned me to death. I suffered from them, but I could still go on living. This was like ice in my heart and I could not recover. It was . . . I can only put it like this . . . it was a crushing, slow petrification of my whole being. Yet, if you had not killed the child at the same time, I might perhaps have forgiven you. Yes, that is possible. I am incapable of bearing resentment for long. That must be due to a certain lack of will power which has been my curse in many other instances.

Half-way along the road, I turn back and retrace my steps."

"Captain Bruckner," I say without anger (because the atmosphere of this room tonight excludes even the temptation to become angry), "Captain Bruckner, you are accusing me of a crime, though what you are speaking of is only one trivial, unimportant occasion. Any number of things happened to André afterward and must be taken into account! Can you really have forgotten?"

"Everything began on my terrace, by that block of cement in which I had fixed a narwhal's tusk that Monsieur Desvaux of the Museum had sold to me."

Aline repeats the gesture she made by the flowering pomegranates that evening; she brushes my hair with a kiss. Brushes my white hair, with her old mouth that age seems to have shrunk. Disgust slithers down my spine like a snake . . . My God, how could I have loved THAT? How could I have found life and pleasure and fragrance in that coffin?

"Everything eternally recommences," says the Captain. "Eternally I shall return to my terrace and eternally a sentence of death will ring in my ears. Sentence of death on a little boy whom you killed, all the while loving him. Sentence of death on a man, executed then and there in the eyes of his wife because the contempt of a child had made him viler to her than a toad."

"Be quiet!"

"Come now," says Bruckner with sudden bitterness, "are you in earnest? Would you prefer that I should really be

48

quiet and that the accusation should come from yourself?
A mere flash of lucidity—a mere impulse of honesty—is
all you need to indict yourself."

"Only one person is guilty of André's death: his father."

"Yes, in one sense."

The folds of his jersey are so straight, so clearly defined
and deep that there seems to be nothing inside it. Aline
gives out that smell of ripe paw-paws which some old men
have. And I? Who am I? How does the world of memory
see me? How do the mirrors see me? I wish no one would
talk to me any more about André and that they would leave
me in peace.

"In one sense, and I would be the last to deny it, André
died because his father's image had been destroyed in his
eyes for ever. He had lost once and for all the face the boy's
imagination had lent him. He had stepped out of the picture, stumbled, and been smashed to pieces on the stones.
Nothing would ever put him together again. Children do
not know how to forgive certain things—they *cannot* . . .
But ponder this with me . . . You don't need to be very
learned! Well, suppose the child had been armed against
disappointment, however cruel and terrible it might be?
Suppose the world had still retained its miraculous quality
for him and had offered him a refuge, that refuge of poetry, of adventure, where no demon can enter and where
one can retreat to get one's breath back in a storm? Let me
insist: suppose he had been helped? Does one defy winter
without woolen clothes? Does one get safely through an

49

illness if one is not nursed, if one is not convinced that the first dawn of convalescence will be the most beautiful on earth? One needs a capital of inner light not to die, and André died because for him there was no longer any light on anything, anywhere, and because, at his age—childhood is only a series of present moments—it was impossible for him to imagine a future of patient waiting. There is no future for boys of seven except a raft floating on the sea of the impossible, escorted by sirens and sea lions and magical manatees—not to mention whales! For him, everything about him had foundered. Every day had carried away something, rotted something . . ."

"All the same, it was not I who . . ."

"It was you. Whatever you may think, the 'Whale's Tooth' barred the entrance to the roads that death had been trying to get through since God knows when. It was the sentinel promising tomorrow, always tomorrow—something other than the dull, daily routine of life in the Galanties's home. It was his assurance that he could get away, that it was still possible to weigh anchor and escape. You spat on the trophy and destroyed the legend; it became nothing but a commonplace purchase—worse still, it became the lie of that old, puerile, over-inventive Captain Bruckner. So all the rest followed. Don't forget that if one falsehood usually engenders another, one honest admission engenders another too. It's like an epidemic of typhoid that spreads if the doctor doesn't check it. Little by little I was obliged—oh, not by you, by my own reawakened sense

of decency—to admit that I was only a paltry seaman who
had only skippered a paltry cargo-boat and never made
more than paltry little cruises, that I was not having any
boat built at the Morel shipyards (and for good reason: I
was as poor as Job), that the voyage to Madagascar was
only a fantasy, that . . . in fact, all the rest. And Monsieur
Galantie and his wife on the one hand, and Aline and yourself on the other, finished off the work of demolition. For
example, remember Flamingo Island! I mention it to you,
not with any bitterness, only with sadness . . .

"If, on one March afternoon, you had not felt an urgent
need to have a little time with Aline, somewhere far away
from me (maybe the idea came from her, it makes no difference) and if you had not decided to take André along
with you as an alibi, if Flamingo Island had remained for
him that inaccessible paradise one had to merit by staying
alive—might he perhaps have been able to survive knowing that his father was a thief and a drunkard? Better still,
might not perhaps he have buried that idol of a father in
his mind, buried him in the Flamingo Island of glorious
resurrections? And then he would have found the will to
go on waiting . . . Everything would have adjusted itself . . ."

On the Island, the afternoon had begun discreetly, on
account of our companion. A purely sentimental stroll. But
I had taken advantage of a moment when he was prancing
about on the foundations and in the ditches of an old fort
to make love to Aline in the shade of the bamboos. She

51

had taken fierce delight in my caresses. The specter forces me to relive that act. The specter is glistening with sweat, and moaning . . .

"Observe that we all have our share of responsibility in the disaster," says Bruckner gently. "It is not because you inflicted a grievous hurt on me that I am not guilty. Alas, I was paying for old frauds perpetrated on other children— on the blacks who always keep something of the child in them—and, little by little, on myself. Wasn't it inevitable that Captain Bruckner should one day revert to the strict truth about himself? Otherwise justice would not have been satisfied. We all have to have our identity cards— that's obligatory, that's the law. You had been the police- man charged to bring me back to lawful behavior. I ad- mitted your accusation; I had deceived people, I had tried to deceive myself. The strange thing—the terrible one too, don't you think—is that that boy went through us like an arrow of light which, instead of illuminating us, brought out everything that was dark in us? Was it to purify us? I do not know. Perhaps. Our impurities left us one by one, as if under the strokes of a magician's wand when what we ought to have done was precisely to keep on deluding our- selves. To lie, when lying was a good deed and helped to keep a pale sun still shining."

He sighs.

"Yes, the 'Whale's Tooth' should have remained the proof that there was a fabulous and friendly ocean on which a fabulous Captain Bruckner had sailed. As long as

Captain Bruckner remained a hero of adventure, and adventure itself retained its allure, André could hope for a magic fairway on which he could sail, safe and serene, away from all misfortune. And, also, once again, I emphasize that Flamingo Island should have remained inaccessible to him: a haven for later on, a kind of treasure. One does not readily accept dying when one has a treasure to look forward to . . . Six months go by for a child like one single day for us. Imagine all that had fallen to pieces for him in one day! Death became the only means of escape. After all, it was death who was generous and it was life who had been the stingy one . . ."

V

We had returned from Flamingo Island just at what my
mother used to call the hour when the sun goes bankrupt: it
turns meek, as if willing to come to terms with its creditors.
I felt thoroughly ill at ease. I regretted what I had done.
The moment we had set out, I had realized this expedition
was dangerous. I reproached myself for having yielded to
Aline's caprice. Why, if her husband was getting suspicious
and our refuge was temporarily forbidden us, we must wait
for better days! Aline was still in a passionate state. She
went on wanting to feel my body on hers and summoning
it urgently. She was deceptively still on her bench as the
boat rocked a little. Her smile was as fixed as a doll's . . .
Hardly had we got home after leaving her at the door than

54

André vanished. More furtively than usual, with that apparently weightless step, just as he did after a scolding from my uncle. It was as if he were hurrying toward silence, as if he felt he were upsetting the order of a world that would not forgive him. And death was following him . . .

"Wouldn't you like us to play a game of croquet, as we did the other day? Or else—we've got time—we might go as far as the landing stage on the west side. You'd see the *Désirée* there, Monsieur Lhoste's two-master that anchored there this morning. She's said to be the most beautiful boat in the country . . ."

No. He was tired. He had a headache.

"What did you think you'd find 'over there'?"

The question had been nagging me. Yet up to now I had refrained from asking it. For the tenth time, I told myself I had been wrong. The islet was now only a piece of land like any other, it no longer suggested anything forbidden, or even unusual. The other day, the "Whale's Tooth," today the smiling mystery of Flamingo Island! It was too much. The world was shrinking. That world which is not our world, which sends messages to a child in a leaf, in a sparkle of mica dust, in the name of a rock and assures him that his sorrow cannot last, that God is watching over him, that there are still magicians.

"What did you imagine you'd find over there? Answer me. Corsairs waltzing with sirens? . . . How stupid of me! I didn't tell you about that fort the Dutch built four hundred years ago, yet you'd have found it very interesting.

Did you see the bullets lying about on the grass? They're very special, they were called red bullets. They were made so that they came out of the cannons red-hot. The expert gunners who fired them used to aim deliberately at the sails and masts of the enemy ships . . . Who knows if the soldiers of this fort didn't sink any number of Arab pirates!"

I could no longer hear his obstinate silence. Each time it engulfed him, I kept thinking there was not much difference between certain silences and death.

"Charlézenn did pretend . . ."

"Ah, at last! Well, what was it that old devil Charlézenn told you?"

"Was he telling lies on purpose? Or did he think he was telling the truth because he's never been to Flamingo Island?"

"You just trust me, will you? *I'll* tell you the truth and no nonsense."

"Charlézenn told his children and me that the shark's cemetery was over there, that all the sharks in the neighborhood come and die there and that you'd find their bones in a big heap as white as snow . . . that's what you see shining from here, just before storms. And in another cemetery beside it there are the pilot fish, those little fish who guide them and who die when they die. And over there, the seaweed's greener than anywhere else and grows flowers that scream when you touch them . . . of course, I didn't find anything at all."

56

"Oh, it isn't always visible! . . ." (Didn't I have to stop the sky from falling too fast?)

"Why's that?" he said, seeming to wake up.

"It depends on the seasons."

"The sea doesn't have seasons like the land," he observed almost sternly. "Even at four o'clock when you suggested my coming with you, I could see that white thing shining against the dark horizon . . ."

He made a disillusioned gesture:

"It must have been the ruins of the fort."

Once again the spider of silence was weaving its web. Mesh after mesh, very fast.

"Don't be so disappointed," I said. "Another day, in May—yes, in May, that's the best time, we'll come back to Flamingo Island. That's a promise. In a motorboat, this time."

"Yes." (He hung his head.)

"Without Madame Bruckner. *She* doesn't believe in all those things. Perhaps that's why the two fabulous cemeteries hid themselves from her eyes and therefore from ours. The sea is capricious and easily offended . . ."

"Without Madame Bruckner, yes," he insisted.

He raised his head at last. I wondered if, in spite of our precautions, he had not dimly realized what existed between Aline and myself. He dared not look at me in the eyes.

"Are you happier now?"

I waited for the music of a child's world to begin to

sound for him again! But not a rift in the silence! He was moving away already, seeming almost transparent, with death following after him. When he reached the door, he barely turned round; engulfed in a chill shadow.

"Come now, André, you mustn't be so sad! Why make such a tragedy over something that really isn't worth it?"

Two days later Aline had hung her mauve scarf with the white spots on the thickest of the four shrubs on the terrace. Bruckner was paying a visit to some relatives in Jamalac. He had left by the mid-day motor bus.

Could I not have done without that woman? If I had been single-minded, if I had thought only of André, I could have saved him. I know I could . . .

VI

What makes me sure is the very fact that not one of the children I meet now is in the least like him. My great-nephews, for example, whom I see at the rare reunions of this family which has broken up in the course of the years and whose homes the "niggers' lawyer" enters only through the back door, after carefully wiping his feet, seem like beings from another world. Does progress explain everything, even though it has advanced at a great rate in our island, in spite of the inevitable lag behind Europe? Too fast for me, who feels lost in this new age. Is the poetry of childhood no longer of a kind I can attempt to understand?

Obviously, in the nature of things, I myself have grown

remote from that period of time to which my heart incessantly recalls me. I am a little dazed as I watch the film which I project for myself and which contains so many blanks and involuntary cuts, as well as being blurred. Everything about it seems dim and old-fashioned. People of my age have been thrust out of Eden; they look back and they recognize nothing. What old Creole or Indian nowadays, the equivalent of Charlézenn, would still dare to imagine, and to tell people, that sharks come to die, mourned by their pilot fish, in a fathom of clear water off Flamingo Island? And what urchin would listen to him? They set up an anti-aircraft searchlight battery on it during the last war and it has remained there. No more bullets in the grass, no more bamboos where one was quite astonished to find the blue and gray "Virgin's bird" reputed to be an incorrigible landlubber. Nothing of the old days any more. A clean sweep.

This sharply defined difference between André and the boys of his age whom I know. Once again, is it solely due to the passage of time in a world that has so radically changed its aspect? I cannot believe it. Was he not, even then, a little boy apart, with his head full of moonshine, assailed from morning to night by some indefinable menace, summoning a thousand mediators who, as soon as they appeared, betrayed him? I suppose this must have been so and I have no doubt that death was on his heels: that is something one can sense *and I often sensed it*. It was death that plunged him into those meditations that were so profound as to worry even Emile Galantie, bluntly insensitive as he was. No one had any doubt about it. Perhaps that was why no one knew how to love him. There are daydreams on which one cannot launch without a special grace. It is like an anointing that separates you from all others. What could confer it on you but the hands of silence, of death? The intimacy with death which, for children, has no name, and glides toward them so gently that it inspires no terror?

I ask myself sometimes: was he abnormal? Might he have been only a mentally retarded creature had he grown up—like that boy who had had meningitis when he was four and whom I nearly adopted at a moment of my life when I felt abominably and utterly defeated? When I ask myself that question, I am up in arms as if someone had struck me. Luckily I promptly thrust it out of mind. That is impossible! He was not that little animal, doomed to the slaughterhouse.

Nevertheless—nevertheless certain memories keep whispering in my ears. Whenever those voices speak to me, they fill me with anguish. I want to leave the house. Go far away, no matter where. "Yet there was this, there was that." A shutter bangs. The wind has risen. The storm is descending the hill on steps of crimsoning rocks. The fatal clarity that precedes the first flash of lightning.

Moreover, these children of my nephews baffle me. Their precise speech, their ingrained sense of mechanics and almost of mathematics, their realism. They are not the type who would demand boring stories to keep them alive. They are healthy and robust. One has no apprehension that the slightest gust will create havoc in their whole being or that they will shatter, like crystal, at a shout. Yes, they are happy all right! It is probably on account of that happiness that we hardly know each other. I avoid them. Try as I will, I cannot help feeling a certain bitterness when I see them enjoying themselves so freely. My thoughts revert to my own poor boy. Lightheartedness is the anchor of the dancing boat of childhood and the bark I meant to guide through the shoals was never able to anchor itself on the shores of fairyland. It had been badly launched and its ability to float was highly uncertain; it needed the absolute, the preposterous . . .

It is so hot, that the shadow at the foot of the trees is episcopal purple. Not a sound, not even the noise of a bird. A ton of cotton-wool on either eyelid; one breathes in cotton-wool; one sweats sodden cotton-wool. The wind is getting stronger up on the mountain and over the sea. The shutter bangs, then bangs again. Once again. A third time. The gale of questions. I want the truth at last. To understand at last why I was able to do nothing for that child. I have loved a stranger to whom I too was only a stranger.

I bring up the idea of alcoholic heredity and promptly repudiate it. It would caricature the image I want to preserve. It would imply a taint from birth. The purple shadow at the foot of the mangoes has been violently rolled up. Immediately, there comes that crackle of sizzling stones. The lightning shows me the face of Fernand Joliet, red against a flaming background. His obdurate seeking for a life beyond the limits of this one is common to many drunkards. To live, to love, is somehow to escape from the infernal circle he has drawn round himself and in which he is imprisoned. If he were a poet, he might perhaps break its spell; he might enjoy his vice as a kind of bartering exchange between fate and himself ("You have given me mud and I have made gold of it") but he is only a commonplace maritime insurance agent who makes a hash of most of his business. Moreover, he reckons up his limitations with scrupulous exactness. It is because he knows them to be too strict that he has taken to drink: to try and breathe an air beyond his narrow horizon. He drinks and he dreams. Alcohol is his serum against reality, against the truth about himself—against his pettiness. But no one ever dreams alone unless he is very strong. Because the dream is incommunicable, one tries desperately to communicate it. Is it not in those mist-bound realms that one has most need of a mirror to convince oneself of one's own existence? Consciously or unconsciously Fernand makes his son the repository of those long daydreams in which he walks upright and dignified and almost splendid. A mirror silvered with innocence: what better one could he find? Even a woman who adored him could not give him so much. He models the child, that piece of fine clay he can transform into any shape he wishes. But never, never must André be able to judge him or to see him as he is; be able, for example, to grasp the reason for those heavy shadows of decrepitude under his eyes. He carries on his play-acting till his head reels and when he can stand the strain no more, he weeps over himself in the night.

Along with all this, he has the faith of a fetishist. There is nothing he does not see as an omen of good or evil. Without meaning to, or without realizing how well he does it, he teaches his son to decipher the dangerous hieroglyphs of allegory. Moreover, it is essential to him to be an object of pity. So he must talk day after day of his cross and invent his own executioners. The halo of the father! The halo that others win and wear differently. His sense of paternity has become preternaturally acute, precisely because he has betrayed it. The halo of martyrdom!—as I myself vainly sought that of fidelity. The colored people to be delivered from oppression and insults, the trade unions, the revolution. Wise men do not use that inflammable material to make fireworks to dazzle a child's eyes as André's were dazzled every morning. Everything that concerned his father seemed wonderful and threatening, as if tinged fiery red. Not only a superman but a slaughtered victim, whom he would love doubly: for himself and for his suffering. Happy my nephews' boys to whom the future speaks only in plain, everyday language. To André, it speaks only of revenge, of the dream at last coming true, the dream defeating the truth and reigning triumphantly in its stead. Moreover, Fernand Joliet never wearies of stimulating that imagination in which he rightly sees his son's, at any rate momentary, safeguard. He stuffs his head with fantasies. He creates miraculous images for the child that symbolize his own quest for the miraculous. Captain Bruckner's "Whale Tooth" symbolizes the glorious salvage of the wreck: a man who, one fine day, will give up drink without any suffering, without even having to make an effort of will. (And, for André, it is the guarantee of some liberty to come that has hitherto been denied him—a liberty that will be reflected on his father's happy, reassured face.) And Flamingo Island is the refuge one has not the right to approach for the moment but which will welcome one later, a haven where sharks have become poetry and peace, where sorrow is hushed and separation blotted out in radiance . . .

So much lightning! The storm is bursting now from all quarters. It is not yet raining, but from every object what looks like the steam of sweat rises toward the approaching deluge. The sea seems to have passed into the clouds. The world is dissolving and re-creating itself, the mountain and the trees and myself and my memories. I am watching Fernand Joliet weep. We are face to face for eternity, are we not, Fernand?

He implores me to forgive him. He tells me that here is his child, that he passionately loved him, that his degradation has not rebounded on him, that in spite of everything, the misery of drunkards should be respected. He assures me that, in Madagascar, he was terrified every night that a small, familiar ghost would come and haunt him.

"Put yourself in my place. One manages to convince oneself that it is in sin itself that there lies the seed of redemption. At other moments, one maintains a cantankerous silence: which is just the same thing."

The rain . . .

VII

For a while, once the first five weeks were over, it was possible to believe that André's grief was abating. At moments
he displayed a certain gaiety. I must correct myself: an ap-
titude for gaiety. But the change was perceptible. There
was a green acacia on the road. I told Aline—who jeered
unmercifully: "He's coming closer to us. I shall save him
from his father and from everything . . . you'll see."

Nevertheless, since his double disillusion, he had taken
to talking about his father again with desperation—I can
find no other word; sometimes with a vehemence for which
he had not prepared us. "With insolence," Emile Galantie
said. Was it to avenge himself for his misfortunes, a kind
of resort to magic? He no longer lived in our midst. He

had taken refuge in his silence. He made one think of those pearly shells on the reefs that close up if a mere cloud passes over them and take a good quarter-of-an-hour to reopen again.

In vain Captain Bruckner had made his reappearance after being in eclipse for several days. André, who had formerly been that purring little animal wanting to be stroked, slid away from under his hand. Bruckner threw me pitiful glances. It is true that he had more or less lost the thread of his stories. He would commence one timidly, break down and be unable to get going again. He sighed, as he dealt the cards with no enthusiasm. Emile Galantie was getting furious. His old man's rages were like the red lamp in a photographer's darkroom. You could see the hitherto invisible features suddenly appearing sharply defined on the plate. What! (he smote the arms of his wicker chair) Was he never going to get a glimmer of gratitude out of that child? It was certainly due to him . . .

"I've been played up too often. My life is nothing but an overdrawn account of affection . . . They squeeze the mango, they chuck away the stone—and goodbye! I've given away too much, lent too much without security. I've pushed my patience as far as it will go. After all, there's got to be a limit! . . . At every step, I bark my shins against the shadow of Fernand Joliet and I'm fed up with it! He fills the entire house . . ."

"I implore you, do calm yourself!"

"Everything here reeks of drink and dishonesty. Fernand staggers about all over the house."

68

"Please, Uncle, please. This child might hear you, understand what you're saying . . ."

"I don't care if he does. Ah, if the fees weren't so high at the Jesuit boarding school at Gros-Bois, how gladly I'd send him there! After all, he doesn't require anything but a plate and a bed. The affection we have for him is the last thing he cares about . . . His damned father! He addles my brain with his father . . ."

"Emile, will you do me the favor of restraining your language!" (Marthe.)

"Mind your own business, will you? Children are out of *your* province. You've nothing whatever to say on the subject. If you'd even had so much as a miscarriage in the course of your existence! . . . But no . . . just a barren desert."

"And who, I would like to know, is responsible for that?"

"Shut up."

"Come on, answer . . . It's easy to accuse my ovaries when you're the one I've good reason to suspect."

I put an end as best I could to the quarrel which started up another day in almost identical words. I told my uncle: "Let things take their course, you're wrong to be so offended. This kid's still too shattered to realize that you love him. He's still floundering among his memories, he can't shake them off as quickly as that. Judge him in a year, in six months, when he's settled down."

"Settled down! Do you believe that possible? We don't count, we never shall count for him. We can die for all

he cares! He's in Tamatave. He's anywhere you like; not
in our home. It doesn't suit either his tastes or his feelings,
Emile Galantie's house . . ."

One of his lean shoulders jerks up violently.

"He's a chip off the old block. He's got the gift of in-
gratitude, it's in his blood. The things Fernand's done to
me! You couldn't reckon them up if you tried! I've been
fleeced and devoured to the bone, but I went on giving
and lending. Coming to his rescue, getting him out of
trouble day after day, knowing very well I shouldn't get
so much as a word of thanks in return. But, you see, he
was the son of my favorite sister, the only friend I ever
had in the days when the family still meant anything. If
she'd lived long enough, maybe I wouldn't be where I am
today? Maybe I wouldn't have committed the one and only
irrevocable folly of my life which was to marry your Aunt
Marthe? . . ."

Once again that furious twitch of one shoulder, always
the same one.

"Ungrateful, yes. And later on, he'll be a drunkard in
his turn. My sister Elise's husband was already drinking
when they got married."

Emile Galantie hurt me when he spoke like that. Probably because he was expressing my own uneasiness? This
child had taken such a place in my empty life—empty in
spite of Aline—that I was weighing up his future as seriously as if he were almost grown up. I could have hit my
uncle to silence him. But what difference would that have

made? An obstinate echo—in myself—repeated his threat, amplified it, made it resound with implacable certainty . . .

"*He'll* become a drunkard too . . ."

"Do stop!"

"It's something that's passed on remorselessly. Not only through example but through the very blood . . . Remorselessly!"

. . . I no longer go to Mass because I have no hope. Yet from time to time I go into the church. This generally happens late in the afternoon. It is like a craving for a glass of water.

For a long time I tried to fight against what I called my masochism which drove me to install myself at the lower end of the side aisle, on the right, where the walls are covered with *ex voto* tablets. Now I no longer resist. I sit down and soon I am surrounded by figures weaving a slow, sad, touching dance. "In gratitude to Mary for the cure of my child" . . . "My daughter was dying. I prayed and she was cured (12th July 1906)." . . . "To Jesus and Mary for the cure of my child" . . . Children emerge from the walls, one and all white, one and all luminous. I forget that many of them became old men like me and died after spending their declining years prudently accumulating more mud to carry down to the delta of death. They surround me with an eternity of youth. Everything is pure and clean. The building is filled with silence, with the

smell of candles and lingering incense. I am like a boat
being lifted little by little off the sand by the tide. I feel
my throat swelling—slightly. There is a vague taste to
the saliva that I swallow with more and more difficulty. I
tell myself that I will not weep, and yet, every single time
. . . Then I see him among the white band. He does not
look at me, does not even make a sign to me. I see no one
but him. There is a sudden trickle of oil over my dried-up
soul. The faint sound of distant singing. That is all. His
image vanishes. He has not told me that he loved me. That
is as it should be. For I cannot hold a child's hand without
trembling idiotically. My great-nephews, when, by chance,
I want to take them for a walk, laughingly decline. "I bet
you go all sideways, like a crab." How could they understand how much they hurt me? That's how I have always
gone all my life, sideways. I have lost everything. My very
family receive me only because they are thinking of my
will which they believe to be a richer legacy than it is.
Ah, my children, if I had been other than I am, perhaps I
might once have saved a child's life and I would not be this
grim, unsmiling man who frightens you . . .

One morning, my uncle struck him. The blood rushed
to my head but I restrained myself; and ever since I have
been desperately lonely and depressed. Did I know what
bond I was signing? And did I know that it was his regret
for his childlessness, the face of years and years of disaster

and disappointments that Emile Galantie was striking when he struck that child? Just as I endlessly pursue a phantom, so he endlessly rebelled against his thwarted desire for paternity—against the phantom of Marthe as a young woman who had promised him fulfillment. All that was contained in that small, fleeting figure . . .

"Will you shut up once and for all about your Papa? I don't want to hear him mentioned again—ever. Put a gag in your mouth if necessary. Do you hear what I say? . . . This is my house and I don't propose to listen to you telling me what Fernand would or would not have done had he been in my place. I don't have to be judged by him. In any case, he's not worthy to judge me. One day you'll know he's not worthy of anything—and why. Shut up."

Like a sensitive plant that closes up if you even come near it, he fell silent. But that continual self-control on the verge of tears! And when anyone touched him, that tremor, that abrupt start, as if he had been caught doing something wrong.

April 1928 was a month of cyclones. There were two of them, all the more deadly for being delayed, and another which aborted in continuous warm rain that fell for several days on end and finally rotted everything that was already long mildewed. At one place, a beaten-down eucalyptus had transformed the whole smell of the world. When a woodcutter arrived at last to saw it up and remove its branches, that green, sugary smell became heavier still. It permeated our clothes and clung to our skin. We moved in an enervating, oppressive atmosphere, in air too dense to breathe. It was like looking at life through a frosted pane.

André was thoroughly at home in it. Perhaps he was really happy during those weeks? Forgotten, Flamingo Island and the Whale's Tooth . . .

"Can you smell it? I just love it!"

He kept going up to the eucalyptus tree, returning to me, then going back to it.

"I wish it would never go away."

"Do you want to kill me with migraine, little boy?"

"With such a lovely smell?"

He was smiling. At last! A light kindled at the bottom of a well.

"In the courtyard of my house there were two even bigger eucalyptuses. The biggest in the whole world . . . Do you remember my house?"

(I did not tell him that he would never go back to it, that it had been sold to the College Braspart to which it now formed an annex.)

"My father told me that birds never built their nests in it; they'd very soon have been just as if they were drunk . . . When I had a cold, Mama used to pick an armful of leaves and make me a poultice of it . . . It's *so* long ago!"

I did not laugh at this "*so* long ago." I could feel the weight of the past behind him, however badly I describe it today. Already he divided everything into two parts, like

74

an old man. Was it because he was soon going to die, that some instinct warned him of this and that the imminence of death created this impression of distance, this dizzy sense of looking back very far?

"I only met your Mama once. I think I've forgotten her."

I had conceived the idea of writing to her. Surely she would grant me some token of affection for her son, a letter or a postcard? But it was true that I hardly knew her because we had not visited her, even before her divorce. I had to have some rough idea of her, so as to decide what note to strike.

"Tell me, what was she like?"

"I don't know."

No emotion in his eyes. On the contrary, a touch of hardness.

"Oh, *she* won't come back! She's gone forever."

"Come, come, how can you know that?"

"If she loved us, wouldn't she have come back when they were trying to put my father in prison?"

"Perhaps she didn't know? . . . Couldn't you send her a letter to tell her? I'll help you to write it. I've got her address in Durban now."

"No."

"But you do think about her sometimes?"

"No, never. I've told you: she's gone forever."

He looked me straight in the face. Still that faint hardness.

"It's better for my father."

Had he witnessed something that had hurt him? Or had
Joliet been unable to keep his matrimonial troubles to himself at those times when a drunkard has to unburden himself at any price and convince himself that he ought to be
pitied—to accuse others so as not to accuse himself?

"Mothers always come back, André. No matter when.
Some day or other you'll see her again."

"What should she come for? She doesn't love me."

"I'm sure she does love you."

Emphatically he shook that head whose hair Charlézia
had cut too short. No denial could have been more absolute.

Those cyclones had been a boon. When the wind had
decreased a little and I took him out wandering through
the ruined orchards, I found a small core of astonishing
strength in him. He ran about, all smiles, among the uprooted trees. He got himself covered with moss and mud.
At last he had come to life and was behaving like a normal
human boy. Did he recognize a certain affinity between
his own lot and the devastation all about him? And was
he thinking too of that revolution his father was always
talking of and which would surely be like this chaos? No
doubt I am attributing to him a lucidity of mind he did not
possess. Nevertheless, this spectacle of nature in ruins intoxicated him; he was at home in it, in *his* world. He was

really and truly walking; he was really and truly alive . . .
He brought back some little twigs in a basket.

"What are you going to do with them, my boy?"

"I want to keep them."

"Right, we'll go and ask Charlézia for a vase."

"No, no, I shall press them in my geography book."

"Between the pages on Madagascar, I bet?"

Torn foliage; strange sisters of the wind and rain.

VIII

After the cyclones came an appalling famine. People of
my generation still remember it. Hunger stalked the island.
Piercing stares as you passed. Knife-like stares. Stares
which followed after you, aimed at your shoulder blades,
or which came toward you, pointed at your stomach.
Wherever you went, all those people, all those stomachs
which hated you for having eaten. I can see them now,
those processions of unemployed going from door to door,
no longer even capable of begging, at once threatening
and frightened. In particular that one in which the men
were carrying a Malabar woman's golden-yellow sari on a
bamboo pole by way of a banner. They were shouting that
her twins had died of the hardships and that God would

78

multiply them a hundred thousandfold in his vengeance. Like everyone, I dreaded a revolt, even while I kept assuring myself that these poor wretches were too weak to attempt anything of the kind. From time to time, the woman herself would take the lead in the procession; half-naked, her flabby breasts hanging down nearly to her stomach. She would howl and curse—and at moments, roll hysterically in the dust—until the police, outraged far more by her obscene attitudes than by anything else, would hit her with belts and truncheons to bring her back to reason. Then she would utter raucous moans, rather like the calls of a seabird in the mating season.

The sugar canes of the coming harvest had been three quarters destroyed. Rice and flour as well as lentils and other dried pulses were lacking. No more imports from India or anywhere else. The port was practically closed to shipping; a cargo-boat had sunk right in the fairway and the continual heavy weather was holding up the work of the dredger sent from South Africa. Everywhere, total and voracious destitution. The Governor had requisitioned stocks of manioc from the factories with the idea of distributing them to the victims of the disaster in place of rice and bread. But this manioc was generally rotten, for the roofs of the granaries had been badly damaged—and how could everyone's needs be satisfied? It was true that the children of the woman of the sari had died of starvation, and it was true that other similar deaths had occurred.

In my free moments, I supervised a relief center. In my

free moments: for Emile Galantie would never have permitted his clerk to desert the office in the rue Mahé for
any reason whatsoever. Anything which had no connection
with the work there was of minor importance. He had
insisted that this center, a crumbling shanty in the middle
of a path bordered by paw-paws should not open its doors
till five in the afternoon. Did I remind myself that the poor
people who awaited my arrival in a great, solid group had,
most of them, eaten nothing since the day before? No
doubt I told myself so; but all I gave them was lofty pity
not love. At the sight of me, an extraordinary tremor ran
through the crowd, like the flickering of a lizard in a ba-
nana tree, and I felt myself pierced by dozens of burning
glances. I always turned round in the doorway before going in. Out of bravado. I was frightened. Every time, I had
that impression that something was being plotted behind
my back . . .

Two clerks assisted me, two young mulattoes paid by
the "Emergency Benevolent Fund." Under my supervision,
they distributed the manioc and the scanty rations of dried
pulse, as well as a lump of lard which had to last five people
for a week. Why did my assistants so often grin derisively?
Was it merely out of defiance? To keep themselves in
countenance faced with this crowd which was simmering
with suppressed violence? Or was it simply unconscious-
ness? I remember one of them as a kind of demon. The
taller one, with the delicate fingers of a pianist. He would
shamelessly fondle the women, making coarse remarks all

80

the while, under the eyes of their husbands who were too frightened or too harassed to protest. I reprimanded him time after time but with no success; he began again the moment he thought my eye was off him. After eight days, I sacked him. But for eight days I had been a coward; for eight days I had counted on his aid in case of attempted violence; he had prudently armed himself with an old-fashioned revolver.

That manioc which exuded a pinkish, sticky liquid, those haricot beans swarming with weevils, those chick-peas which could be hours on the fire without being really cooked . . . Whenever I think of them today, I am plunged back again into the stench of that hovel in which I imagined myself to be acting as a brotherly benefactor. I can smell once more that mixture of rancid grease, vegetable mold, and sweat, breathe that air filled with the dust of mildewed starch. I stamped hastily printed food-cards and ticked off names in a register, humble work for which no one else had offered his service.

Occasionally (to show off?) I lit a clay pipe or lost my temper—quite amazed at my managing to shout so loud across this sluggish sea of misery. And eternally, eternally, the manioc and its secretion and the lard which melted in that vapor-bath heat; eternally, those famished specters. When I shut the door again and a constable arrived to take on sentry-duty for the night, it was like seeing a swarm of tiny fishes scattering when one throws a stone. In a hundred glances rage, fever, rebellion, flickered wildly and brilliantly for a moment, then relapsed into the depths of despair. Ah, if only I had loved those men! If only I had understood what they were demanding of me! But I belonged to my class and I belonged to my race. I knew nothing of material want; the house where I lived was intact or very nearly so; I was going to be a solicitor, a prosperous career awaited me, life was only just beginning . . . Too late now for regret, my good man!

Parallel with the official organization, three private committees had been constituted, one of which, the League of Charitable Ladies, wives of administrators, sugar planters, engineers, doctors, lawyers, etc., comprised the entire *Almanac de Gotha* of the island. Some young girls, nearly all of them looking for husbands, worked for it; at that time doing charitable works was the best means of acquiring a halo. Once a week these ladies distributed plates of hot rice, salt fish, and potatoes with their own fair hands. That particular day—Saturday afternoon—the white Lady Bountifuls appeared in silk dresses . . . But what gives me the right to be virtuously indignant? Didn't I form part of the whole setup as secretary of the local branch? Was I any less indifferent or more sincere than the others? Any more genuine? Did I drag even the shadow of a cross in that Passion we pretended to alleviate?

Aline Bruckner aspired to be one of us. Belonging to the League was a certificate of good birth, as well as of distinction, not to mention of being well-off. The Captain himself made no secret of the personal satisfaction he would derive from it. It would bolster up his self-esteem, my uncle said, make everyone forget his financial and other embarrassments, and he would re-enter—or rather enter—the world of the rich and respectable.

"Yes, my dear young friend, the fact is that Aline would very, very much like to take part in your laudable activities. Be kind, and make it easy for her: that shouldn't be difficult for you, should it? I'm quite aware they haven't so far thought of her, but . . . Naturally, she insists on bringing her contribution on the financial plane . . . yes, yes, that goes without saying. I shall break into our small savings. I shall do it gladly . . ."

"Let's go halves, Captain Bruckner. Won't you agree to that? Now, now, don't shake your head: you'd be doing me a service. I definitely want to contribute my mite to the League and this would be the most discreet way of doing it . . ."

I was trying to get myself forgiven for the episode of the "Whale's Tooth" and what had followed. But I was going the wrong way about it.

"No, certainly not. I can manage very well. Besides, I received an increase in my pension just before the disasters. I would like to give Aline a present."

All that loaded on the back of poverty! A shorn sheep . . .

"You see, Aline has a heart of gold. Nothing would please her better . . ."

"Consider the whole thing fixed, Captain Bruckner. You can tell her so. I'll deal with it tomorrow . . . These ladies have begged my aunt Marthe to join them; Aline will take her place. You know my uncle! He's always opposed to anything that's called good works . . . Which hasn't prevented him from sending quite a big check to the Government Fund."

"So I read this morning in the paper."

"For goodness' sake don't think it was he who had that printed!"

"Such an idea never occurred to me! Monsieur Galantie belongs to the cream of our society: his gesture served as an example . . . That was how I interpreted the paragraph announcing it . . ."

The shorn sheep, poverty, has bloodstains on its back. They are growing larger. Aline Bruckner is here beside me. She wears a pearl-gray suit and gray shoes as well. All this is a very pretty gray; it must have cost a lot. She is elegant, in spite of her rather heavy figure. Really alluring; that vivid bloom, like a winter rose, that women have when they are nearing forty and suddenly shoot up a high flame, even brighter than in their youth, before their fire begins to die out. Several men stare at her—the husbands of some of these ladies, whom they have accompanied—and I tell myself they are stripping her with their eyes. I am conscious of a vague pride. Ah, if only Captain Bruckner could absent himself tonight! If not we'll go somewhere, no matter where, Aline, won't we? I feel true desire for you. The need of you . . .

Wives of engineers, doctors, lawyers distribute the rice, the salt fish, the warm potatoes. They wear gloves. It is I who gave Aline hers (she told Bruckner she had patiently saved up for them). There is a little spot of lard on one of them and I shudder. I hate the poverty that has bloodstains on its shorn sheep's back, that poverty that has also splashed such expensive gloves with lard. I want to go off alone with Aline. I want to leave it all behind me, the ladies and their cackling and their donations and this ledger where I endlessly check off the names of destitute people. I dream of undressing Aline, taking off the gray suit that has revealed new contours of her body to me and her new smile and her new shape. I am infuriated by the concentration with which she is playing her part. Couldn't she spare me one look? Couldn't she brush her arm against me now and then?

Rice, fish. Rice, fish. Rice, fish.

Enough of this!

Rice, fish, and two potatoes per head . . .

Can't you hear me? Enough, I tell you! I don't care a damn for the fish and rice of the poor. Stop bothering me with your food-cards and your stamps and the whole paraphernalia.

"Your name?"

"Martial, Jean."

"Are you married?"

"Yes, Ma'am."

"Your wife living?"

"Yes, Ma'am."

"How many children?"

"Four."

"All alive?"

"Yes, Ma'am."

"Have you a receptacle to take your rations away in?"

"Here, Ma'am . . ."

Hail fellow, well met with poverty. With poverty in a black skin. Why should it be respected in such a dark skin. Is it not Cain who is begging at this moment? Abel is this condescending monarch under the tree of life.

"Is *that* your receptacle? How can one eat out of anything so dirty! *Pigs,* my dear, just look! . . . And they propose to get themselves educated! They propose to raise themselves up to our level one of these days! . . . Positive *pigs.*"

The smear of lard of Aline's glove has spread over the whole world. Saint Abel's lovely, brand-new gloves . . .

"They really are the race of Cain! Just look at those sly, insolent eyes . . . My good man, do you want me to call the constable to teach you to lower your eyes?"

Aline, let's get away from here. These rich women get on my nerves, these beggars get on my nerves. *You* get on my nerves too, with that suit you keep tugging at all the time, as if it embarrassed you, as if it were made of some fabric too precious for you. I would like to thrust my hands in your pockets and tear them and slowly, slowly let my fingers creep over your warm flesh till they reached your breasts. Far away from here! In the fresh air, in the sea wind.

86

Won't they soon reach the end of all this rice and this stinking salt fish? We shall never be able to get away by ourselves for a moment before we both have to go home to dinner and be parted all night. Never, Aline. That suit has taken on your perfume. In the maddening smell of this hovel, every time I look at you—yes, I have only to look at you—I am aware of your perfume and your alluring body. We should be so happy on Flamingo Island at this hour when the bamboos are so light that they look as if they would fly away if they were not held down by their shadows. Here I am in hell, surrounded by all my demons. I am afraid of charity being my true vocation and of realizing it too clearly. I do not want to know myself. I want to live, Aline. Save me. Take me away. Find some excuse and let us go off together. Banish this temptation I have to supplant Fernand Joliet, to be the genuine revolutionary he never was and never will be. His little boy, *my* little boy, is asking me to replace him as the hope of this crowd of colored people. To brandish the torch of liberty in his name. I have neither the strength nor the courage for that, Aline. Nor the desire. Put your hands over my eyes, speak, prevent me from seeing, from hearing . . .

"Your name?"

"Deokynanum Seetaram. Two children."

"Your card?"

"I've come for my sister too, Madam. Sandranath, you know. The one who had her legs broken in the first cyclone."

"Have you her card?"

87

"No, Madam."

"Well, go and fetch it then. Nothing without a card. We know you, you race of Cain! No one is better at shamming than you are. Born liars, the whole dirty lot of you!"

The last portions of rice, and darkness falls. A stormy sky over there, toward the table-lands of the interior.

"You're not going home straight away, are you, Aline?"

"You know perfectly well he's waiting for me. He's become very jealous these days . . ."

(The relief constable: "Goodnight, Madam. Goodnight, Sir.")

"Goodnight . . . Cigarette, Constable?"

"Thank you, Sir . . . The other night there was a fellow prowling about for a long time round about here. If he turns up again, I shall shoot."

"Well, shoot in the air then! It's some poor devil who couldn't even manage to break in the door."

"Must we separate so soon, Aline? I love you so much in your gray suit!"

"Not otherwise."

"Why, of course. Most of all, otherwise . . . You know quite well what I mean."

"You think of nothing but that!"

"I'd like to undress you—very gently . . ."

"I'm not saying no. But . . . where could we go?"

"Suppose I took you back to the rue Mahé? I've kept a key . . . We'd be quite undisturbed. The big sofa in the waiting room . . ."

88

"No, no! I'd be too afraid Monsieur Galantie might come back to the office for some reason or other."

"At this hour? He'll be having dinner."

"No, really, I assure you . . . Let's be good tonight; it would be better."

"Oh, Aline, must we? . . . I've been dreaming all afternoon of making love with you. Listen. Suppose we just simply go down to the beach, where there are all those big ravenalas?"

She hesitates. But I know she is going to accept. I have kindled her desire.

"You will? I want you so terribly tonight."

She seizes my hand. I feel the same emotion that I felt just now when I imagined myself tearing her jacket and caressing her through her warm blouse.

"Yes," she says, and her voice is almost harsh. "Never mind where . . ."

The darkness is astir. It is not the wind; it is the darkness itself that is throbbing with her breathing, with the rise and fall of her breasts, with the sexual vibrations between us. Above us, the darkness is urging on a storm, step by step, toward the south; here below it is urging on passion. Reed-buntings come and go, silent and patient. They have lost all their volatility in this sensual, suffocating atmosphere. They form a fifth element of mingled silence and movement, death drifting toward resurrection.

"You look marvelous in your gray suit. All those gentlemen were devouring you with their eyes."

"Were they?" (Her perfume seems suddenly to have grown more intense.) "Did they think me attractive?"

"Extremely . . . But it's got to end there. I'm more jealous than your Captain is."

She laughs.

"Idiot! I'd really have to lose my head to forget that I love you."

"You're going to show me you do as you never have before. Say yes?"

That perfume that becomes still hotter as desire mounts in her. We turn at the end of the path between the pawpaws. Barely more than a hundred yards and we shall be on the beach. Tonight the sea is only audible as a tiny muffled splashing: a sea in love.

"Tell me, were you satisfied with your afternoon?"

"Very satisfied."

Her whole being thrills with pleasure . . .

"No disappointment? Did those ladies accept you as you wanted them to?"

"Yes, I think so. I got any number of compliments . . . Madame Lartigue has invited me to tea next Wednesday. Up to now she barely acknowledged me when I bowed to her . . ."

The sand, so warm under our feet. Here are the ravenalas. "Traveler's Trees." I used to play Robinson Crusoe among them when I was a child. Tonight I enter under cover of the ravenalas as if stepping on blissful velvet. At last I take Aline's arm, no one can surprise us here. I abandon it at once for her waist. She has unbuttoned her jacket and her blouse. The velvet of the ravenalas pricks my skin like a thousand tiny needles.

"My hair . . . for goodness' sake be careful of my hair . . ."

IX

The moment Emile Galantie greeted me, I knew from his voice that he was furious.

"You're back very late!"

"It took longer than we thought it would. Those poor wretches poured in from everywhere . . ."

There was a brief silence. He looked at the clock and shrugged his shoulders.

"Do you know that rioting has broken out? The police have had to open fire. Outside the Government Building. People have been killed and wounded . . . You'll do me the favor, as from next week, of renouncing all your activities for the Benevolent Fund and, in particular, your famous Saturdays. As long as the aid isn't distributed by the police themselves, it can only serve to inflame hatred. If the whites are generous, it's because they can afford to be: that's what these men and women think. Don't expect any thanks from them, just the reverse."

"There's some truth in that," I said, trying to sustain his threatening gaze. "But there's also some falsehood . . ."

"Falsehood?"

He went on staring at me. As if he were measuring and judging me.

"There's no falsehood," he said slowly and sternly. "No one can give unless he has something to give. And if he has something to give, he has a thousand or more times enough to live on. You're provoking the revolution by imagining you're making your unemployed and your homeless wait patiently for better days. Bring food to those people at the point of a gun or don't offer them anything at all. Mark you, I know these people! . . . What are you going to tell them on Monday? Yes, you, with your charities. That their leaders were in the wrong? They'll tell you to go to the devil. Believe me, revolt's already rife all over the place. That sort of news gets round among them faster than all our telegraphs."

He sat down. That wicker chair, almost in the center of the drawing-room, was his imperial throne. He had only to bang his fist on the table for everyone to be silent.

"You will therefore inform the authorities of the Benevolent Fund that they can no longer count on your services."

"Let me go on for a few days," I replied. "Then they'll

93

have a little more time to replace me: it isn't a particularly sought-after job . . . Let's say till the following Monday."

I was thinking of Aline. Would she retire too if I asked her? Or would she stay on? I did not like the idea of her going over there without me. Messrs. Blanchet and Gébert and others had looked at her much too eloquently . . .

"In any case," I went on, "I might arrange to have a detachment of police outside the Center, at least for the next few days, just to impress the crowd. You could help me."

"Starting tomorrow," said my uncle furiously.

"That's impossible!"

"Are you living in my house or are you not?" (He made his chair creak.) "There is one fact you do not mention. An organized riot has occurred, the supreme insult to us whites. I will never consent to be the tacit accomplice of these blacks for whatever charitable motive. I'm not in the habit of letting myself be trampled underfoot. You will resign. I've already told you frankly what I thought of all this twaddle."

"All the same, Uncle, I've first got to . . ."

"You've first got to obey me," he growled and his lean fists were like those flint objects they show prehistoric cavemen grasping in pictures. "Let Lartigue and Gébert and their wives and the rest carry on with their pious clowning if they want to; they'll never conciliate the blacks. We've got to display our strength, that's all, and in no uncertain manner. No doubt they'll send us a cruiser from South Africa if things continue to go badly. Fine! It'd be

still better to present the rioters with the only possible
united front of the whites: toughness. It's the only thing
they appreciate. When we had to stand up to the Rivière-
des-Créoles rebellion in 1885 I was your age and believe
me I wasn't sparing with my riding-whip. I'm not in the
least sorry. Now the whole business is starting all over
again. Defiance and the whiplash. It goes in cycles. As long
as the whiplash follows hard on the defiance we shall be
safe. Otherwise . . ."

His two fists remained clenched, bluish under their knots
of swollen veins. He clutched his armchair as if to assert
his absolute proprietorial right over everybody and everything here: his imperial power.

"I've taken on responsibilities," I said timidly, sitting
down opposite him.

"You'll put an end to them."

"You're asking me to damage my good name! I repeat,
it's impossible."

He crossed his legs. A touch of melancholy flickered in
his eyes.

"On the grounds of equity, it was impossible for me to
choose you as my successor," he said. "Everything pointed
to Fernand. I had promised his mother I would. He was my
godson. Nevertheless, it was you for whom I paved the
way . . ."

He added, with a promptly repressed warmth: "Because
you were made for this position and because I was fond of
you. Because you were like me in my youth."

95

He averted his head. When he turned to me again, he had recovered his impassive mask. Only he was panting a little, as on the day he had talked to me of his sister Elise, his confidante, and of what his life might have been had she not died all too soon. He must have felt humiliated by his confession.

My thoughts were still busy with Aline. There was no question of my opposing Emile Galantie's wish; my future depended on my obedience. But what would Aline say? I was revolted by the idea that she might continue to appear at the center, that men other than myself might meet her, talk to her, and perhaps pursue her. What solution could I find? I was stabbed by jealousy. I must, at all costs, think up some stratagem. Such as to persuade all these ladies to retire *en masse*. That was the only way out. I would set about it tomorrow morning. If necessary, I would invent the discovery of a plot and lay great stress on the brutalities the blacks were planning to inflict on them the following Saturday.

"So that problem's solved," said Emile Galantie. "Now you've got another on your hands."

He paused for a moment.

"I expected you earlier. You've got to calm, or try to calm, your pupil and make him go to sleep. Neither Charlézenn nor myself have been able to . . . As for your aunt!"

"What!" I exclaimed, leaping to my feet. "Is he ill?"

"It's not very serious, don't worry . . ."

He spoke without conviction. I was quite sure he was minimizing the truth.

"You're the only one who can do anything with him. Since we don't count in his eyes . . . or only count as policemen."

"Explain yourself! What's happened?"

He silenced me with a gesture. It had cost him something to say what he did just now and he was furious with me for having heard him say it.

"Obviously I was wrong. Bruckner and I were both wrong, to talk about this riot in front of him—not to have noticed he was listening and that no doubt he was feverish already . . . but I'd just had the news on the telephone. But really! This hysteria! this madness! What are we coming to? Pretending the revolution was the signal that his father had come back, and that we were trying to keep him away from him . . . What insanity has come over the boy? Fernand never has been and never will be a man in any sense of the word and this child's got to know it—as soon as possible. It's vital. In a rebellion he'd no more act like a man than he would in anything else . . . I'm counting on you."

Everything that still reminded me of Aline, her scent on my hands and in my mouth, was suddenly forgotten. I was alone, face to face with myself. How quickly pleasures have to be paid for! Here I was, solely responsible for a sick child whom I was going to have to make still worse. Despised human misery was taking its revenge. Bruckner was taking his.

"Uncle," I said, and my throat was dry, "aren't you afraid it might be typhoid?"

He drummed on the ebony table with increasingly nervous little taps.

"They've announced the beginning of an epidemic," I insisted. "You know that as well as I do. I've just been told of three fresh cases not far from our house. Severe ones . . . The Health Service is having the houses in the street disinfected."

"You're talking nonsense," he muttered angrily.

He stood up in turn, dominating me with his white head that was higher than my own. All his will was in his eyes, to calm me and perhaps calm himself.

"Utter nonsense! A little temperature of 102 degrees and you promptly get the bit between your teeth . . . A mere bout of malaria, that's all! He's subject to it. Fernand warned me. We'll know where we are tomorrow . . . Believe me, I'm much more worried about this overexcitement which has got to be checked at all costs. It's bad in such a little body. His nerves have been overstrained far too long."

"You must call in Dr. Malleret," I said emphatically. "It's essential. This is something more than malaria, something more than nerves . . ."

"For the moment, the main thing is his father," said Emile Galantie, heavily stressing every word. "We've absolutely got to finish with him. He will never return to this country, understand that. I shall use every means to stop him; he's done me too much harm already. So what's the good of tolerating the presence of his ghost here and,

98

what's more, his heroic ghost? Our duty to André is to do everything to prevent such a thing happening again. I implore you to act for the best."

He sighed noisily.

"If only you'd come home two hours earlier, perhaps we might have avoided this distressing business! Now I've been obliged to slap him, yes, twice, in spite of his fever to bring him back to some semblance of calm. Your aunt is no earthly use in such circumstances and I was afraid it was going to end in convulsions . . . But you were regurgitating charitable platitudes in the company of our imbecile socialites, you were playing the ministering archangel, dispensing crumbs . . . now go and see the result for yourself!"

Aline and the ravenalas . . . I hate you, Aline.

X

I entered on tiptoe. Charlézenn's wife, Charlézia, promptly
left as silently as I had come in, like a small, thin breathless shadow. The bedside oil lamp gave a scanty light.
André appeared to be asleep. The greater part of my
anxiety left me. But then I suddenly saw his fevered eyes,
like two dark lanterns. They would not stop staring at the
door with the gaze of one who would never humble himself or yield or even soften. Could I manage without too
much difficulty—without doing too much harm—to dissi-
pate the fairy tale this child had invented for himself? He
had started at the sight of me. It was not me he was expecting. Or only if someone were with me—I had gone to
find his father at the scene of the riot and I was bringing

him back to him . . . Alas, I was arriving alone and I was saying nothing!

I sat down beside him. I was desperately searching for words. I wished I were a thousand miles away. All the same, wasn't he panting a little less? Surely his breathing was easier! He had understood! He was beginning to find a reason to account for it.

"Well, André, whatever's up with you? All the children in the world have been asleep for ages at this hour! What are you staring at with your big eyes all bright and feverish? I'm here, you trust me, don't you? I love you, you know: almost as much as your Papa does . . ."

I felt his forehead. It was burning, with dense sweat on the temples. His temperature must be at least 104°. The dread of typhoid suddenly preoccupied me to the exclusion of everything else. It kept surging up and dying down and returning, with the movement of those waves I could hear through the closed window-shutters. I tried to reassure myself. They had announced three cases at Grand-Bourg. Well, what if they had? It was too soon to talk of an epidemic. Ridiculous! *We* didn't drink polluted water. We practiced hygiene. These cyclones and their consequences had not greatly altered our way of life. "You keep brooding over these notions of illnesses from morning to night. You're the one who needs a doctor. You'll end up by being really mad. A little while ago, it was tuberculosis you were afraid of. You always have to imagine that death and misfortune are prowling around those you love." It was true, but I could not do much about it. Ten years earlier, when the emigrants had brought us yellow fever from India, had I not developed a veritable complex? I used to watch my parents all day long, with an absurd tightening of the heart if my mother stayed in bed later than usual or my father complained of those giddy fits to which I knew quite well he was subject. Tonight, at any rate, it was essential to be cold and objective. Apparently, all we had to deal with was a bout of malaria. Emile Galantie was perfectly right. Tomorrow, it would have subsided. What remained to be overcome was the nervous shock. It must be done patiently. "Look here, your Papa . . ." Obviously, one mustn't depict the real Fernand Joliet except in a very round-about way: the very first thing to do was to demonstrate the impossibility of his immediate return . . .

My hand on his forehead. How I wished I were a saint with the power of healing. "Hope can do all things." It was my mother who had affirmed that, only a few days before her death. "Hope can do all things and from up there I hope to be able to watch you living and to guide you right up to the end." The phrase was like a knell of doom to me. I had nothing tonight to constrain hope, the daughter of charity, to smile on me. On the contrary, I had insulted her . . . Had not my hand stroking that forehead just been caressing Aline, with the long sensual caresses that precede the final act? I had lost all right to hope, even the right to pray for it. On the contrary, what my fingers were imprinting on André's forehead was an ac-

102

cursed sign which offered God a target where He could strike me most surely and cruelly to punish me. In this religion of give and take—of the immediate passing on of responsibility from the guilty to the loved one—in which I believed without knowing why since it ran counter to my upbringing, "I will return good for good and evil for evil," I was condemning this child by my presence rather than comforting him . . .

I rebelled at the idea. It was unthinkable to take God for a monster, to want Him to belie His very name of creator. But I revolted without much conviction. A furtive animal within me was frightened.

"There, there, little one, don't be so restless. You must go to sleep. Everything will be better tomorrow, you'll see . . . Perhaps you caught a chill the other day when we were out on the jetty watching that beautiful sailing-ship from the Albion Dock, do you remember?" He could not stay still for a moment and kept giving convulsive starts. A ray of light filtered in, the yellowish glow of a big lamp. The door opened noiselessly. My uncle and aunt were standing on the threshold. It was so strange—so ominously strange —to see them together on this night of anguish! If they were observing a truce to their hatred, it could only be because the situation bordered on tragedy. The apprehension of disaster had brought them together again. My uncle shook his head. His eyes were screwed up in the light of the lamp whose wick was turned down to its lowest; all hardness and obstinacy had gone out of them. He made as

103

if to enter, then changed his mind and went away. Marthe followed him almost immediately. The door shut again. For some moments I heard them talking in low voices in the passage but I could not catch what they were saying.

André's restlessness had calmed down at the sight of them. Was he dreading a brutal remonstrance like the one in the afternoon? For a moment, he huddled up under his sheets. Now that the danger was passed, he relapsed into his fever with a kind of relief.

I extinguished the bedside lamp.

"I'll lie down beside you in this armchair—we'll go to sleep. You know quite well you needn't be frightened of anything when I'm here . . . Look, we're both going to dream! I'm going to dream that it's tomorrow and you're well again—and you're going to dream that . . . that I'm bringing you a nice present to celebrate your recovery. Let's do that, shall we?"

"No. Light the lamp again," he said. Then he added urgently: "I want to see the door."

I pretended to laugh. "Well, that's a funny idea! Why do you have to keep an eye on that door? Do you think Father Christmas is suddenly going to pay you a visit? It's not the right time of year for him! Or perhaps it's Captain Nemo, come straight from the Nautilus just to see you?"

"I don't want to go to sleep. I want to wait for my father. He'll be coming any moment to fetch me."

"Now do please be sensible!" (I had begun stroking his

forehead again.) "Your Papa wrote to you ten days ago: has my little boy lost his memory? He was very well, he sent you hugs and kisses." I hesitated. "He was saving up penny by penny so that you could come out and join him next year . . ."

He hardened. Even his breathing was harder.

"He's come back."

"Come back?"

I laughed again, unconvincingly.

"He's waiting for you to be bigger before he comes back. If he knew you were feverish and that you were acting like a crazy boy instead of going to sleep, he wouldn't be at all pleased."

I went on as fervently as possible:

"I've never lied to you. If Fernand had come back, wouldn't we have told you so at once? We'd both have gone to meet him at the station."

With difficulty, he raised himself on his elbows.

"Please light the lamp again."

"No, André."

"Light it again, if you love me."

I lit it again. His face was streaming with sweat. I wiped it with my handkerchief. There was still some of Aline Bruckner's rouge on it. There was Aline's scent in it.

"Please do something for me, go over to Captain Bruckner's . . ."

Had he recognized that scent? Anything was possible. We did not, so to speak, receive any woman other than

Madame Bruckner . . . In any case, it was of no importance. But I felt embarrassed.

"What do you want me to do at Captain Bruckner's?"

"Ask him if a boat arrived from Madagascar today."

"But, look here, my boy!"

"Perhaps you haven't heard about it? *He* knows all the
ships. I'm sure he'll tell you, yes—that a boat anchored
this morning—that my father was on board."

His elbows collapsed. He fell back on his pillow.

"We'll ask him tomorrow when he comes to ask how
you are. Meanwhile, I want you to leave that door alone
and go to sleep."

"Why don't you go at once?"

"Because the Captain's been snoring for ages by now!"

"Is it so late then?"

"Very late."

He was utterly panic-stricken.

"I can't understand how it can be so late and my father
still isn't here. I'm sure something's happened to him . . ."

He pulled himself up and went on: "Unless Uncle Emile
won't let him come in?"

"Now, really," I said, feeling my nerves beginning to
fray. "What reason would your father have for coming
back? Do you think he wouldn't have given you notice
of his arrival?"

I clasped his hands in mine, holding them tight with
all the tenderness, all the fatherliness I had in me. Oh God,
don't force me to murder him! Let the truth be made

known to him kindly, without any cruel shock, above all
may I not be charged with the telling of it . . .

"It's this business of the riot that's misled you. They
were wrong to talk about it in front of you. A riot—that
isn't the revolution, André. No, it's just a momentary dis-
order and this one wasn't very serious. A little brawling
and it was all over. You told yourself, didn't you . . .
Come now, if it had been directed by your father, things
would have been very different. He's a real revolutionary.
He's methodical, he's got courage. When he does something, he sees it through to the end."

Those hands. Why did they suddenly feel so hard, as if
they were nothing but bones.

"When your Papa starts up the revolution, you'll know
it all right. Everyone will know it. If it were he tonight,
wouldn't you hear them shouting in the streets 'Long live
Fernand Joliet'? All the black folk in Grand-Bourg would
be shouting it till they were hoarse . . ."

Like the gust of a monsoon, I could hear the voice of
Emile Galantie: "Fernand's nothing but a drunkard who
only pretended to be a political agitator to blackmail me—
that's what the boy's got to know. It's imperative . . ."

"That's not possible, Uncle. Don't you realize it would
kill him?"

"I order you to act for the best. Do you live in my house
or don't you? Fernand will never set foot on this island
again: I shall prohibit him by every means at my dis-
posal . . ."

107

I let go of the small, bony, fever-hot hands.

"I'm not going to tolerate the ghost of Fernand Joliet here any longer, get that into your head. His heroic ghost, which is even worse . . . This masquerade's got to stop."

"I'm going to tell you something. You don't know your Papa well enough yet. If you knew him as I who've been his friend for so long—we were at school together— you'd know that . . . that he's not a man who acts lightly. That he's also a very kind man who would never let poor devils be killed in a riot that was doomed to fail in advance. Of course, he's preparing the revolution. Of course he is, because he's told you so. But for later on, when the right moment comes. Much later on. With him, there won't be any brawling and killing; he won't have any need to use violence . . ."

Lying was going to my head and making me feel as dizzy as if I had been drinking. Was I lying well? Did I seem sincere? Was I being kind enough?

"In any case, if you want Fernand to be happy over there in Tamatave, you'll shut your eyes, you'll obey me . . . There! Now at last you're beginning to go to sleep. It's the best of all remedies, to sleep . . . to sleep . . ."

The bony hands on the sheet. So much like the hands of the dead! What was it that smelt so strongly of lavender in this room? Ah yes, Aline, my handkerchief, perhaps my clothes. Was it not also the suffering of children—of this particular child?

XI

Dr. Malleret had dismissed straight away the notion of typhoid or any other nefarious illness. Merely an ordinary attack of fever, quite common in growing children. He had come in a cart, his Overland being out of action as it frequently was, and he smelt of horses. This odor was very strong in the closed room.

"Give him aspirin, there's not much else you can do. In any case, stop the quinine; it'll only make him tired and do him no good. No diet! Let him eat as much as he likes. Anything he fancies . . . Eh, my little lad, mustn't starve yourself, you know! What you need is to lap up life in any shape or form as a little dog laps up a bowl of milk. Now give me a smile."

"You see!" said Emile Galantie to me grimly. "I told you what he'd say . . ."

I had had trouble in getting him to send for Dr. Malleret after André had been ill five days. My uncle thought it was throwing money out of the window. He had given in but he could not forgive me for my insistence. The doctor's re-assuring diagnosis had increased his annoyance with me. The tone he used to me was clear proof of it.

"A mere trifle, and you lose your head and imagine the sky's going to fall! The clouds can never be black and omi-nous enough for you, can they? Anyone would think ex-pecting the worst corresponds to some deep need in your nature. Typhoid? What next? Why not the plague? For your New Year present, I shall give you a medical dic-tionary." He threw a harsh glance at André, who tried vainly to avoid it, hypnotized by those accusing eyes like a bird by a snake. Emile Galantie sighed and turned to Dr. Malleret.

"So it was only a storm in a teacup . . . In our day, Mal-leret, we didn't fly off the handle so easily! We had a good lump of solid sense in our heads . . . Of course your answer would be that if some people didn't panic at the sight of a thermometer, you wouldn't possess a little yacht, three houses, a motorcar, and certain other things and, by God, you'd be right!"

He laughed. His laugh was even more grating than usual. Malleret and he were obviously the same age. They had been schoolboys together and close friends, I believe.

TH E *Isle*

Life had driven them somewhat apart; there was a suppressed, but emphatic rivalry between them, each striving
to be the most important personage in the district. There
was also mention of a certain matter concerning a woman,
of Dr. Malleret having been something more than a friend
to Marthe Galantie in his youth. (How impossible I found
it to imagine those two old bodies making love!) In any
case, the affair had not been very serious, and their mutual
affection had persisted, with only a drop of vinegar in it
. . . The two men were dressed eternally in black alpaca.
Both had mustaches.

Malleret's laugh, clear and generous, echoed my uncle's.
The latter was thinking of the fee he would have to pay.
Paying was something that invariably annoyed him. His
creditor inevitably became an enemy to whom he had to
administer a passing scratch.

"Tell me, Malleret, have you turned jockey in your
spare time?"

"What d'you mean, jockey?"

"Haven't you got a nose, my good friend? You smell of
horses as powerfully as if you were one yourself! . . . I only
said jockey out of charity."

"What d'you expect?" (the doctor recovered his jovi-
ality) "What with my car which gives me more trouble
than my wife and daughter put together and these Hindus'
carts that are never cleaned and spend the night with the
horses that pull them! . . . Pooh! I bring a healthy smell of
the turf and your little lad here thanks me for it. You like

111

horses, boy, don't you? Your uncle was a great betting man in his youth."

"Oh, before he became a solicitor and learned the value of money!" he added. "Now he always backs winners, he bets on dead men and wills . . ."

"Your fees take into account the hire of the cart and driver and what the repairs to your Overland cost you, I presume?" asked my uncle in a bittersweet tone.

"Naturally!" exclaimed Malleret, slapping him on the back. "You wouldn't wish it otherwise?"

He added at once, seriously: "All the same, I want to talk to you."

"Oh, do you? And why, may I ask?"

My uncle drew himself up stiffly. He stared defiantly at the doctor. "What's all this mystery? Don't go inventing difficulties where there are none, for heaven's sake . . ."

"One moment," said Malleret, "this is not the place. And besides I've finished with this little boy . . ." He patted André's cheek in sign of farewell and we left the room. The child followed me anxiously with his eyes, like a sailor trying to decipher the signals of a lighthouse at night. Why was I accompanying those two men? What was being plotted? What was going to be the result of this secret conference?

When the door was shut behind us, Malleret said brusquely: "Galantie, that kid's very ill . . ."

He raised his hand to anticipate my uncle's retort.

"No, I haven't lied to you. There's no question of ty-

112

phoid or any other form of pestilence. You can be absolutely certain of that, so sleep in peace. All the same, this
isn't all that much pleasanter. Your little fellow is quietly
and unobtrusively dying. That's absolutely certain, too . . .
He needs comrades, amusements . . . I don't say 'he ought
to have them,' I say 'he's got to have them.' Obviously you
have difficulties about schools and he's too young for
boarding school. What can you expect? He needs to be his
age, that child, whereas he's living a precocious, unnatural
life, cast adrift all alone into this perpetual silence that's
enough to drive anyone crazy and into an old people's
world. I don't for one moment doubt your kind heart and
your patience, you know that perfectly well. But we should
be irresponsible if we shut our eyes to the facts. In any case,
the very first thing he needs is affection. I'll be precise:
motherly affection."

"The mother has thrown away everything: husband and
child and decency," said Emile Galantie drily.

"So I've been told."

"As to the father, I've packed him off to Tamatave and
he'll be there for a long while yet . . ."

"I'm aware of that too."

"What do you expect me to do?" growled my uncle. "I
can't work miracles! You talk of affection. Little André has
his cousin who practically never lets him out of his sight
and is as kind to him as any mother. I've nothing else to
offer him."

There was quite a long silence. It seemed to me that Dr.

Malleret was staring at my uncle with undisguised contempt. Here, out in the wind, we were at last spared the smell of horses.

"Dear Madame Galantie will rise to the occasion," said the doctor in a tone more interrogative than affirmative. "She will consider it an honor to replace that absent mother."

"*She?*" My uncle burst out laughing. "Good heavens, you must be dreaming!"

"She's a woman," said Malleret firmly. "Take my word for it and pass on my request to her."

My aunt had remained in her room. She had long ago blotted out Henri Malleret from her universe and not for anything in the world would she have consented to see him again.

"I'm not a person who gets worried easily," said the doctor. "Rather the reverse. But I'm obliged to speak frankly to you: this child is undermining his health and this business can only end badly . . . A kid needs other things besides food and drink!"

He hesitated.

"I know the misfortune that happened to his father—the misfortunes, if you prefer. They've left a terrible impression on him. He's a child who's all nerves and unhappiness, you can see that straight away. Some solution's absolutely got to be found to the problem. Return of the father: we can exclude that. Impossible, anyway?"

"Impossible," said Emile Galantie, drier than ever. Aggressive.

"I understand . . . Nevertheless some affection and some companionship other than the affection and companionship of his cousin are vital to your André. He needs what amounts to a mother. I repeat: what amounts to one. Why!" (he was getting worked up) "your great-nephew simply cannot go on living as he is now. He is imprisoned in this great empty house. Every day that goes by destroys him a little more. One feels that he has been deprived of something essential. You've only to look at his eyes . . . A wretchedness that positively wrings your heart."

"I'll think it over."

My uncle thrust his thumbs into his armholes, giving it to be understood that the conversation had, in his opinion, lasted long enough.

I accompanied Dr. Malleret to his hired cart. He was already stepping into it when I decided to question him.

"Doctor, can we be sure this child hasn't any tubercular tendencies?"

"Practically sure."

But why had he that anxious look? Why that troubled, almost surly expression? Just now, hadn't he blinked?

"Obviously, I can't make an *ex cathedra* pronouncement. It would require a thorough searching examination. What makes you think of T.B.?"

"I don't quite know. I . . ."

I was groping for words. I felt I was being vaguely criticized—unfavorably criticized. "So the dumb have decided

to speak," Dr. Malleret must have been telling himself and
thinking it was shabby of me to have kept silence in front
of my uncle for fear of his sarcasm.

"Look, Doctor, I often get the impression that André has
a temperature, not, of course, as high as today but . . . He
nearly always has hot hands and unnaturally bright eyes.
His depressive state—is that the right expression? . . .
Could his depressive state be one cause of it?"

"If he had a mother, she'd have taken his temperature,"
he said with smothered anger. "At least I'd have had something to go on! As it is, we're talking wildly, we're merely
conjuring up possibilities. You couldn't be more precise?
Mere impressions won't get us far . . ."

He shifted his instrument case from his left hand to his
right, returned it to his left, and went on in a more agree-
able voice: "I'm practically certain your anxieties are un-
founded. One has an instinct, otherwise medicine would be
no more than a grocery business. Diagnosis counts for
something, after all! It's a kind of nose or a kind of an-
tenna. I've made no secret of what I thought. Your
cousin's illness is his hopeless, joyless existence and as regards that, the doctor has, unfortunately, no say in the matter. Yet if that skinflint of a Galantie is prepared to pay for
Richaume to give him an X-ray, that would certainly be far
better. We oughtn't to neglect any possibility."

He held out his hand to me.

"There, there, the old Daddy in me is more touched than
you might think by your affection for that poor puppy. Life

started to maltreat him early . . . *I've* had five kids, my boy. I adored them. Now they hardly give a damn for me and treat me as an old idiot. That's normal, and I don't bear them any grudge for it."

Once again, he held out his hand, forgetting perhaps that we had already shaken hands.

"Don't let your imagination run away with you more than you can help. For my own part, I can't repeat it often enough; the danger here isn't physical, it's moral—mental. Sentimental, if you prefer. What has that child in his mind when he daydreams? Answer me that. Does he daydream like other children? That's what one has to consider. Bad, when a boy of seven drags himself about all day under a heavy cloud . . . All right, talk to Galantie about your T.B., but make it quite clear to him the idea doesn't come from me. If the radiograph turns out to be negative, as I hope, and he can attribute the error to me, he won't fail to abuse me . . ." He broke off, then added: "Hold on, this is probably more important: talk to him about boarding school too. I said just now that your cousin was too young for that and it's true in one sense. But I'm sure that anything would be better than his present existence. He wouldn't do badly with the Jesuits at Gros-Bois."

The cart moved off with difficulty, with a slow heavy creaking of wheels. The sparrows did not disturb themselves for the broken-winded horse which never raised its head. They only flew off in a flock at the sound of the

117

driver cracking his whip at the corner of the street, no doubt from sheer force of habit.

"My impression, Doctor Malleret, how can I convey it to you? The impression that he scarcely belongs to this world, that he does not solidly inhabit his flesh, yes, that's it—that too intense an emotion would kill him. And there is that perpetual shadow brooding over him. You have not seen it, but *I* see it. A shadow taller than he is but which has his form and his face . . ."

XII

"You'll inform your aunt of our exchange of views with Dr. Malleret," my uncle said to me that afternoon in his office. "Personally I'm not going to risk it. I should be too afraid I might laugh if I had to pass on such ridiculous suggestions to her. Marthe in the role of a mother! That would create a sensation, even in a circus . . . Give her the message, all the same. If necessary, stress the fact that in my eyes the whole thing's nonsensical; maybe that'll give her a slight inclination to do it."

He was brimming over with a strange, cynical gaiety. Had he not detested alcohol, I might have supposed he was drunk. All at once, he was another man.

"I can prophesy this: if your aunt makes it her business

to look after this child as you ask her, instead of leaving him to Charlézenn's wife, you can add another infant martyr to the ones on the calendar . . ."

"You slander her," I said, forcing myself to turn the thing into a joke.

"Oh, do I?"

"It's true she doesn't feel at all attracted to André or to children in general. But aren't you judging her too severely? Sometimes people only need an opportunity to make them change. Perhaps up to now she's been afraid of your criticisms and that's made her withdraw still further into her shell? You must admit you don't treat her very tactfully! There's never been a child in this house before. André's arrival has created a new situation for you, hasn't it? The same applies to her."

He had listened to me impatiently. With a barely concealed animosity. He rapped his desk sharply.

"Even if you go on making long speeches in that vein, like a barrister at the Assizes, you can't prevent facts from being facts. Marthe, a woman? What nonsense! A tomb, and I've rotted in it. She doesn't exist, except as hatred, and icy hatred at that. The other kind at least would be a sign of life . . ."

I knew that this was his favorite topic and that there was no stopping him once he was launched on it. Was he right? Was he wrong? I had no means of judging. In any case, he would not have brooked the slightest contradiction on this subject. I contented myself with reminding him that Malleret had been very positive. I added that if André could, in some way, come to represent for Aunt Marthe the child she had longed for as ardently as he himself had, his home could only be the happier for it. He tried to interrupt me. "Don't say that," but I went on.

"You're both suffering from the same thing, from one and the same unhappiness. This companionship you've missed so much, she's missed it just as much as you have. Why shouldn't André be a pretext for the two of you to be reconciled? You could throw a bridge over the gulf of time. Cross it and everything would be transformed . . ."

He interrupted me vehemently:

"Don't say that, whatever you say! Don't ever put that idea in my head—the idea of consoling Marthe. Once and for all, and whatever you may think of me . . . If I saw that Marthe was becoming attached to André and that her affection was returned, I could no longer endure that child. Is that clear? I could no longer stand the sight of him. I, and I only, am the one who has suffered from the emptiness of my heart. That is something you cannot possibly understand. *She* didn't give a damn about it . . . I tell you, she didn't give a damn about it, she told me so herself . . . It's I who have had molten lead poured day after day into my heart. I hope you'll never know that searing inner silence, never know what it means to feel your very blood becoming silence, your name becoming silence . . .

"I've reached a point where I've shut myself off from everything. Who's responsible for that? And you want me to forgive? For years and years I've been a man who no longer hopes. I've wearied myself out with waiting. I've rejected God, I've rejected life because I've waited too long in vain and grown sick of things, one by one. My house weighed on me like a tortoise's carapace. I loathed my clients—and I couldn't divorce because it was even less permissible in those days than it is now—my clients would have turned their backs on me and I would have had to give up the office . . . I kept on the practice; how could I have lived otherwise? And Marthe was still there, she wasn't dying, she hadn't even a stomach-ache! All that, in order that she should blossom out now? Even if it were a question of a vague, barely envisaged possibility, that would be too much to bear. I loved her once but now I hate her. It would be flagrant injustice. Get this into your head and tell Malleret so if you want to. If Marthe ever became for little André what you want her to be, I'd . . ."

He broke off abruptly. He was ashamed. He was trembling. I knew his rages but I had never known one like this. It was useless trying to persuade myself that he had exaggerated his feelings.

It took him a long-drawn-out moment to calm himself.

"Oh, my mind is quite tranquil! You can try as hard as you like. God himself couldn't succeed in producing a flower from a stone."

He was astonishingly pale and his nostrils were pinched. That was how his death-mask would look. I felt like insulting him, yet also like pitying him. All those years of rancor that were bursting out in a stream of mud. What was the true destiny of this man? Where was he going? Did he still preserve any aim? Did he still love something—his profession for example? his trees and his garden? his house? I very nearly took his hand as if he were a sick man and said: "Come to your senses. You've talked too much, but that doesn't matter. I can take it or leave it." I did not dare. I should never understand this old man. All those violent contradictions in him. Strength and the most despicable of weaknesses. Loftiness and an incredible baseness. And the good he did (for there was nothing I did not know of what went on behind the scenes in his practice) which was promptly spoiled by an attitude of ostentatious, offensive contempt. Who was he in reality? And what had Marthe been to him? Had there once been genuine love between them and was his wife's sterility, or possibly his own, sufficient to explain why they had entered into this darkness from which there was no return? Or else had something extraordinary happened long ago? Had some thunderbolt fallen of which I knew nothing? And would their secret go with them to the grave?

My mind reverted to André since that secret would always remain out of my reach. What was his position here as Emile Galantie saw it? An abandoned child whom he had taken in? After the diatribe I had just heard, I could not understand why or how my uncle could have taken the risk of bringing him into his home. Was it a wager? Did he imagine that he would win his infernal bet against Marthe and so finally crush her? Or had he simply had a craving to hear a child's footsteps, a child's voice, in this house of bitter disappointment? It was the bet against Marthe that had determined him; I could feel it—I had felt it so many times! But then why, five days ago, on that first anxious night, had both of them come to look at the little invalid, as if something stronger than time or hate had suddenly reunited them? What was that thing? A sudden mutual wish to protect? A sudden and mutual love?

They had not entered the bedroom, out of embarrassment in each other's presence, yet they had talked in low voices for quite a while outside in the passage. With no shouting, no anger. Had they found themselves side by side in a dream, reliving a scene which might have occurred thirty or forty years earlier? They had been father and mother for the space of a few minutes; then they had returned to their respective monastic cells . . .

"Come now," said my uncle, "I wasn't telling you anything new, I presume? No doubt I let myself go a little, but Malleret irritates me. He's got the charming habit, ever since we've been neighbors in Grand-Bourg, of regarding your aunt as a misunderstood saint and me as her torturer. Torturer of what? Of my own heart? All I asked was to be made happy. It's what every man seeks—and I am a man like other men."

He stared at me fixedly, and corrected himself.

"I was a man like other men . . ."

He had begun to fidget nervously with a file of papers. He dropped it.

"As for André . . ."

He made an evasive gesture.

"I'm going to write to the Fathers at Gros-Bois. He'd certainly be in good hands there."

Was he using it as a threat? Was he trying to blackmail me? Did he want to revenge himself for having bared his naked soul to me? No doubt he was afraid of being taken at his word. It was quite a heavy expense to contemplate.

"In any case I couldn't get him in till the autumn term. The Fathers make a point of not accepting anyone in the middle of the school year . . ."

"Aren't you afraid that would be far too late? According to Doctor Malleret, the matter's urgent."

"What else do you propose?"

He exploded. Once again I saw that furious man who, a few moments ago, had lost all dignity. He made spasmodic, uncontrolled gestures.

"Appeal to your aunt, then! Appeal to her, I want you to! Do you hear me? *I insist.* Let's see that female ape doing her job at last! . . . If it's on my account she's refrained from playing at dolls up to now, all right, let her play at them now! It makes me want to laugh—to laugh my head off . . . See here, you're to ask her why, in 1912, she refused to adopt that little girl, that little mulatto girl I brought to her? For social reasons, maybe? Because her noble blood would have been humiliated? Or to finish me off? Ask her that, I tell you . . ."

The sound of a client's ring at the doorbell put an end to this painful session.

XIII

If Emile Galantie remained to me, in many respects, an enigma, of my aunt I knew nothing whatever. In any case she was a monster, whether of rancor or of misery. She kept you so obstinately out of her world that, at certain moments, the mere fact of looking at her seemed to constitute prying. Very occasionally, one day or one evening, she would fly into a rage and shout curses and imprecations; then everything would relapse into silence and there would be eight or ten days during which you only seemed to see her from the other side of time, that is, if she deigned to leave her room. All I knew about her—on any kind of external plane—was that for a long time she had occupied her leisure hours embroidering children's leading-strings for a needlework guild (people still talked about "Madame Galantie's leading-strings"). But she no longer did this . . . She was a woman so locked up inside herself, so vacant, that my memories of her are like memories of another life.

I realized at once, when I repeated Dr. Malleret's suggestions to her that there was nothing to hope for from her. Her refusal was categorical. I have to admit that I did not use any ardent persuasion. Emile Galantie's homily the day before had been enough to prevent that. Moreover, I dwelt on an alternative solution which seemed to promise me many advantages. After all, I was only asking the maximum of this woman in order to obtain the minimum: a little *visible* tenderness for André, some token of affection given from time to time . . . She replied that she did not want, at any price, to become attached to him since he was destined to be taken away from us.

"Come now, that won't be for a long time! Fernand can't decently return for two or three years, maybe even more. And there's no question, as you know very well, of sending his son to join him in Tamatave. How could he look after him? Whom could he trust to take care of him?"

I am going back over the course of years. I am inventing our conversation of that morning. In a sense, I am dreaming it. But does not my version express the real truth that lay behind the meager words we exchanged?

After the death of my aunt, I read some notebooks—just little school exercise-books—in which she unburdened her-

self in her thick, exaggeratedly firm writing that was so unlike a woman's. I ought to have been discreet and thrown
them in the fire but I read them. Oh, she never revealed her
whole self in them; she deftly avoided the full searching
glare of the mirror—for example, she hardly ever mentioned André. Nevertheless, our conversation could logically have taken the course I represent it to myself as
having taken. And I still wonder why two people like
Marthe and Emile Galantie, both so exact in the analysis of
their grievances and their frustration, did not find a *modus
vivendi* which would have made their life bearable. Was it
precisely because they were too exact, too thorough?

Our dialogue, as I re-create it now, is a dialogue with the
shade of Aunt Marthe of the "journal" and of Aunt Marthe
as I recollect her—a kaleidoscope of obscurities and hesita-
tions and innuendoes . . .

"All the same, you're not going to pretend that this boy
means nothing to you? That he isn't worth some effort on
your part?"

"Is there anyone to whom children mean nothing?"

"Then explain this to me, Aunt. However much I watch
you, I don't see any change in you since he's been with us.
I've been aware of a certain feeling in Uncle. I admit it was
quickly repressed; he controlled himself as he's so adept at
doing—but the feeling did exist. Why has there been nothing similar in yourself?"

"What do *you* know about it? Can't you look below the
surface?"

"But what *did* you feel then?"

"What's the use of trying to tell you? It would be so difficult—and so useless—to try and explain to you . . ."

A silence within the silence. I lost those notebooks a long while ago. A ray of silence filtering under the stone.

"I've earned the right to be left in peace. I'm permitted to think of myself occasionally, don't you agree? For years and years I did embroidery for children who, for me, had neither faces nor names—mainly for little black children. Doesn't that tell you anything? I grew weary of that work. No doubt because I no longer had the strength to keep up this farce for my own benefit. Because I was too old and no longer felt tied by even the thinnest thread to the world of childhood and children. Life has made me into a coffin. Everything is cold now. My bridal sheets folded away in a chilly cupboard. I no longer rebel except mechanically. I scream so that your uncle may never forget, for one instant, to his dying day, that he has utterly destroyed me while all the time assuring me he loved me . . . You criticize me when you ought rather to pity me. Nobody pities me. Charlézia herself and her husband loathe me because they think I am haughty. If I did not wear this mask, what would people find themselves faced with? A poor, wretched woman . . . I have my pride."

"But I *do* pity you!"

"No, you don't. You don't treat me as an enemy, but you've no real pity. You ought to be sorry for me, you ought almost to weep when you see me avoiding any physical contact with André—a kiss or a hug. My life has been

130

spent in waiting for a child's kiss, in dreaming that a child would come and embrace me when I woke up. A whole century of waiting. Now all the lights have gone out. Why should I try to light them again? I should be punished the moment I yielded to the temptation. Not only would your uncle intervene but I should suffer from watching this new flame flaring up too late, knowing that it could only dazzle me dangerously. Don't remind me now of the past, I implore you. It would be a wicked thing to do. I have drawn the curtain. I no longer have any womanly feelings. I no longer have the slightest maternal instincts, the faintest desire to be maternal. You dare ask me to play the mother? You're mad! If you're not mad, you're crueler than Emile. I no longer have a face. Leave me my mask. I've just told you I couldn't do without it."

"All the same, kindly tell me this: Why did you come to the door of André's room the other night, so upset because he was ill?"

"I was seeing a little animal suffer."

"Without thinking you might be able to do something for him?"

"Of course not. But I did not know what."

"You didn't want to know, wasn't that it? Wasn't it a relief to you not to know?"

"You're right. I did not want to. It was that temptation I was telling you about just now . . . Besides, your uncle was there beside me. Once again, he was making me sterile."

She draws a long breath. Her breast scarcely rises. She is speaking the truth: she is no longer a woman.

"I have grieved too much and too long for you not to allow me to close my eyes when I consider it necessary for my own sake. It is necessary for me today to refuse your request. I should play my part badly and I should be ashamed of realizing I was playing it badly. No, I assure you. No."

A glimmer on the brow of the mummy. On the cheeks of the mummy. A subdued fleeting semblance of light . . .

"Doctor Malleret was in love with me once, no doubt you've been told that? He too led me into the desert. He only pretended to love me—I soon realized that. He consoled himself in a few weeks. A jovial man, as you've seen. He was no less jovial then. Nothing in his behavior has changed. Everything flowed off him like water off a duck's back, nothing upset his maddening geniality. He's always swum with the current and taken the easy way out . . . In my day, one didn't deceive one's husband lightly. I dreamed of having a child by Henri Malleret since I had nothing to hope for from your uncle. He knew it. Good heavens, he must remember it! Isn't it an insult to me to even offer this other child to me—this child which is not his and which, moreover, will go away leaving me lonelier than before and once again vulnerable? I don't want to be caught in the trap. I will never accept—never."

A long pause. The kaleidoscope has jammed. Only very slowly does it begin to function again.

"Do you really want André to become a whipping-boy and be thrown out of this house once and for all?"

"On the contrary, I mean to do everything to make his life happy!"

"In that case, I'm the last person you should turn to. Your uncle would loathe him if I loved him and he loved me. He'd get rid of him as surely as two and two make four."

"So he pretended to me, but those were only words! He couldn't be as spiteful as that . . ."

"With him, words are invariably followed by actions. Emile hesitate to commit some black deed if I am to be the victim of it? You don't see him as he really is. He will do exactly as he has said. Nothing will restrain him. If ever you realize the full extent of his cruelty, you will understand me, though a man always understands another man better than a woman does and is inclined to find excuses for him . . . The lonely emptiness of this house—is it my fault if nothing has ever been able to banish the loneliness! Emile must have spoken to you of a young mulatto girl, Cécile. But what conditions he proposed for our eventually adopting her! It was a veritable death-sentence pronounced against me. All I must give this child was a *material* presence—do you grasp the full import of those words? To be no more, in fact, than her governess! Forbidden to love her or, at any rate, to tell her I did. Why? Because, according to him, that would be disastrous for her upbringing, for her future stability. I was too dull, too

melancholy. Was it not my duty to crucify myself? Moreover, this girl was to be your uncle's sole heiress. I was to
renounce everything in advance, solemnly and officially.
Anyone in the world would have refused. Because it was
a wanton, criminal act of provocation and also because I
would need an income if my husband happened to die before me. And also because I had nephews and nieces who
were expecting a great deal from their aunt . . .

"Cécile died when she was thirteen, far away from us,
in a hospital. Emile blamed me for her death. How was I
in any way responsible for it? For years, for endless years,
he tormented me through her. He drove me nearly mad.
Besides—this was one of the reasons for my negative attitude—I knew that she would be desperately unhappy
with us. That there was no place for her in our ruined
home. Was I mistaken? Is there one today for André?"

"André must be saved . . . he *must* blossom out and be
happy."

"Here? That's impossible."

"My uncle is thinking of sending him to the Jesuits at
Gros-Bois next term. But I don't want him to be separated
from me."

"Emile contemplating such an expense? such generosity?
He's not serious, my boy! He'd sooner let him die . . . Let's
be practical. Why shouldn't Aline Bruckner be this pseudo-
mother of André's for a while, till he's on his feet again?
You've thought of it already, don't lie to me! That would
suit your book so well in every way! I'm quite aware that

she is your mistress. I couldn't help knowing it. I've caught
you two or three times kissing her on Captain Bruckner's
terrace—I was hidden behind my curtains and I am in-
quisitive—it's all there is of the woman left in me. And I
often smell her scent on you; those are things one doesn't
miss . . . They start one dreaming—that's something you
can't understand. Does your uncle know of your liaison?
He's never breathed a word of it to me. He won't see the
slightest objection to what I'm proposing to you. On the
one hand, Madame Bruckner will save him the boarding-
school fees; on the other, she'll help him to drag me a little
deeper still into the mud, for that is what will happen . . .
Go on, ask your fair friend to replace me. She has no child,
either. Perhaps you will be doing her a great kindness:
doesn't she still keep hoping? Who knows, she may be
pinning her hope on you? She's only thirty-six after all . . ."

XIV

That was a very strange interlude in my life, at once richly happy and squalid.

In spite of Dr. Malleret's assurances, I had been very frightened all the while André was ill—twelve days. I returned to the surface with all the eagerness of a diver. And, like a diver, I was so intoxicated by breathing fresh air again that the whole world seemed to be dancing and shouting in my honor. When his temperature went down at last, I was so crazy with joy and gratitude that I almost expected the very mountains to burst into song. I had indeed told my uncle of my apprehensions about tuberculosis but he had laughed at me and, heaven knows, he had been right; I really was too ready to create a private hell

for myself. I gazed at my boy with a fatherly satisfaction.
He was cured! No ill chance would befall him again. I
would protect him against it, I was strong.

Those patient afternoons I spent with him, sitting at the
foot of his bed on the wooden trunk in which he kept his
toys, and talking to him about the coming revolution as if
I were expecting it and longing for it. Proving to him, over
and over again that his father was too intelligent a man,
too sincere and important a leader, to have been mixed up
in the recent riot, that he would leave Madagascar only at
his own time, when events were ripe, etc.—everything, in
short, that I had told him many times but which he loved
to hear me repeat. He would listen to me, happy and serious. He made me think of flowers, just before dawn, not
yet open, with the dew spattering the folded petals that
imprison their scent.

"Do you think he'll come back this year?"

"Something tells me he will. Just a hunch. But obviously
I may be mistaken. It's quite likely that all this will need
some time . . ."

"A long time?"

"Oh, how can I answer you, André? That depends on
so many, many things! In any case, what *you've* got to do
is to hurry up and get thoroughly well again. He would be
heartbroken to come back and find his boy looking so thin
and pale."

A passing cloud.

"I was so, *so* sure he was there the other night, that they'd locked the door so he couldn't get in!"

"Ah, ah! There's that little clockwork engine starting up again with its wheels whizzing round and round in the air!"

"Uncle Emile's so often said he didn't want to hear any-one ever talk about him again!"

"People say lots of things when they're in a temper! And then they forget all about them . . . So don't give it an-other thought."

A silence.

"I was frightened too . . . I wondered if he hadn't been killed in the riot . . . Then I saw you weren't crying and I knew that nothing of the kind had happened. You would have cried, wouldn't you?"

Had his illness left a mark on him, accentuating his need to be protected—his physical need for the support of an older person? Had I, on my side, made so much head-way toward him? What I cherish from those days when he was convalescing is the memory of an idyll. What other word can I use? The idyll of the branch and the silkworm. It cannot be told. What images could convey it? I could see hope reawakening. How can I express it better? I could see childhood returning to a child. During those twelve days when his temperature oscillated between 100° and 104°, he had looked like a little old man. Observe a sick child carefully and you will understand me. Observe him, for example, when his breathing is labored and sweat

makes every one of his features stand out sharply. His face
is the face of age and experience. You have the feeling
that nothing *innocent* can ever live in him again.

That childishness reappeared in him, hesitantly, shyly.
I found myself painting a glorious picture for his benefit.
A bee hummed high in the sky. A jacaranda swayed in the
wind in the depths of a secret forest. "You realize your
father's too splendid a fellow to . . ." I transformed myself into that father by reinventing him every day and
idealizing him. I became another Fernand Joliet, calm and
dignified, rich with my child's trust in me. I would be for
him, without fail, the dispenser of pure marvels. Come,
we will restore the true face of Flamingo Island, we will
re-create it as it was when it emerged from God's hands
for the delight of boy dreamers. Over there, we will find
the imprint of a siren's body to show where she slept, silent
queen of her ring of sand and bamboos. Henceforth life
will preserve forever the smooth warmth of a healthy
skin . . .

"Isn't that so, my boy? Now you are really and truly
my son, tell me you are! Nothing can separate us. You'll
become a man and I shall be an old man but we'll go on
being two companions, two comrades . . ."

Was he ugly as I have sometimes been assured, when
he had not been gone long enough for his image to have
vanished completely from my memory? Anyone who said
so was lying! His face at those moments was so radiant!

"I might have been married and had a boy of your age,

by this time. But I shall never get married now that I've got this fine big lad here . . ."

Did he understand? Or did all that just seem to him nonsense? He was laughing. He had brought out of his treasure-chest the collection of postcards of ships Captain Bruckner had given him and which he had not looked at for some time.

There was only one shadow between us: why had I not taken part in the riot? Hadn't I assured him that I shared his father's feelings about the blacks and would demonstrate it at the first opportunity? Doubtless I should have led them to victory, and, with the police muzzled, the exile from Madagascar could have peacefully taken his homeward road. Yes, why had I abstained?

"Because you were ill. I couldn't leave you all alone."

"That's true . . ."

But he was not convinced. The question was brought up again later.

"You were so feverish that you were delirious. They sent someone to warn me. I rushed back . . . You were expecting me?"

Drift after drift, the shadow receded. Hope shone out full.

The echo of my words in this house, though the sea is loud tonight. The echo of his words. It all has a blurred, drowned resonance. I scan the evening, the night coming up on the west wind. Will a lighthouse at last show its beam in my darkness? All I can see is vague objects, a kind

140

of submarine landscape. Shall I never be able to remember spontaneously what I said to that child and what he replied to me? Remember his gestures, his attitudes? I try so frantically. I deserved to succeed. I dreamed of telling the story of his life; this house should have helped me. A few people might read it one day, perhaps the blacks, and thus he would live again for a moment. But I am well aware it will elude me to the end. Has he left me too long for my mind to be capable still of concentrating? Have I lost my way beyond hope of return? I open my hands again; all I had caught in them was the wind. Soon, doubtless, even the wind will escape me. What shall I be then, I who am so lonely already? I keep repeating to myself, as if I were saying real words: "We'll organize the trade-unions together." I say it emphatically. I try to make the phrase ring with conviction, to give it at last some color. Waste of effort. Did it never have anything but that flat, hollow sound? I cannot admit it. That far-away time I have allowed to die must have been a fairy-tale time. A lie that left an after-taste of honey . . .

"It's a very long task to create trade-unions. It's like planting a tree: you have to wait till it buds, then till it has leaves, and finally till it has fruit."

The language of an old man. And the fairies turn their backs on old men. I must surely have expressed myself differently. In spite of the fact that, in those days, I detested the cause of the workers and called it dangerous anarchy . . .

How those words "but" and "nevertheless" have been

part and parcel of my life! How shall I ever end it with a body and soul at peace?

"We shall succeed, I promise you. There will be great rejoicing. And banners unfurled for your father's return. We shall be on the quay when the ship—the *Ville d'Oran* out of Le Havre—sounds her siren and thousands and thousands of black folk will be all round us, clapping and cheering. Perhaps we shall weep for joy, you and I?"

Trade-unions, golden word, spun out of shimmering cobwebs. Today, now that I have learned to love it, it no longer means anything. It is part of the everyday, commonplace language, in this island as in the rest of the world. Established by law. The black folk are free. I am a dweller on the moon, an old moon, hanging low in the sky, that will soon be eclipsed. I am no longer capable of recapturing, still less of describing, the rainbow magic a small boy could put into the word "trade-union." Neither can I convey that it was once an enchanted world, where two glorious figures stood shoulder to shoulder, bathed in its radiant light—myself and a cousin of mine who had been dispatched to Madagascar for fraud.

The era of fairy tales. The era, too, of the idyll of the branch and the silkworm. The image persists; it keeps recurring and I do not repulse it. Because it makes a counterpoise to the squalor that was about to usurp it. For a moment that kindly breeze blows and, looking back over the long, long years, the sea is very blue, its bosom very maternal . . .

XV

Aline, guiding star of my destiny . . .

What a long way I had traveled since the arrival of that sorrowful little boy who had fired me with reverence for purity! A journey round the world! Then I could not even endure to let my mistress brush my arm when André was with us. Even if there had been that hateful expedition to Flamingo Island, I had repented it bitterly enough. Now we were going to form a trio. He would serve as a pretext, he would act as a cover for our sordid love-affair. A green branch hanging over the cesspool. My spirit had certainly undergone a radical change. This gloomy house had accomplished its work. Yet was this outburst perhaps due to another cause too? Was it a kind of paean of praise to

143

life after the cure I had so passionately longed for? It crowned a period of intense revolt against the narrowness of my upbringing. The death of my mother had only very recently set me free of it. Throughout my entire youth, she had weighed heavily on my conscience. Loving her and reviling her simultaneously, I had avoided anything which might have displeased her. Wherever I went, her presence, severe or anguished, had accompanied me.

Had I known that André's death was already approaching, should I have behaved differently? Oh yes! But am I not lying to myself? Even with the terror of that menace in my mind, should I have allowed myself to be lulled by my body's silence as I have done for so long? But enough of analyzing and ratiocinations! A spider, lurking at night in the midst of his web, might as well try to find one strand of it that had not been deadly to the butterfly! Is not every rain-spangled thread of the snare he spun equally deadly? What does it signify, this puerile desire to decide the real reason why I did this or that, except an attempt at self-justification? I know myself to be guilty, yet here I am, pleading my own defense! I remain, in old age, the wily fox I was in my youth.

I want to pass on quickly. Not to stop and dwell on it. To hurry over that time . . .

Our long afternoon walks to the guava woods of Chamboron and the wild cocks whose hoarse, metallic cries receded gradually into the distance, little by little closing the world around us and leaving us alone—and blessedly content. Those interminable pacings up and down, as darkness came on, under the trees of the headland, with André wandering ahead of us, with seeds crackling under our feet like firecrackers set off by some Lilliputian populace to welcome us, with Aline kissing me from time to time, without the little shadow ahead of us noticing; kisses that were all the sweeter for having the taste of forbidden fruit. The sea, under its diadem of stars was like a watchful presence. But could we not find, at will, the means to be alone together at the house when Captain Bruckner, faithful perforce to those whist games, left us his villa and time to appease our desires? We used to make André lie down on a chaise longue on the terrace. Dr. Malleret insisted (we said) on these rests in the warm breezes of late afternoon.

I asserted that Bruckner was faithful to whist out of necessity, on account of his many obligations to my uncle. But could I be certain that it was not his nobility of heart that impelled him to be so complaisant? Or that it was not, just as likely, contempt? One question arose insistently above all the confusion in my mind: Did he not love André more than I did, a hundred times more sincerely, a hundred times more paternally? I told myself that the idea was ridiculous. I tell myself so still. I offer my mangled life as a proof of it. I implore everything in this house, all these objects that know me, to bear witness for me. But the question sounds louder in my ears than the noise of the waves: Where was the love that is all light, that needs no words, no gestures, no proofs to express itself? Bruckner had lost

André's affection, the placid sea of the boy's gaze where the captain could relive his dream of legendary voyages; and he knew it. He had lost still more during the abortive riot in April when, in front of that child, he had raged in concord with Emile Galantie against "the foolish and criminal pretentions of the blacks, those beggars who ought to be shot." He had even had to renounce the hope of ever winning him back again. He was perfectly aware of that too. I had taken good care not to hide it from him. On the contrary, I had stressed it since it completed my triumph over him: henceforth André was mine and mine only. Yet he cared deeply enough for that little drifting bark and deeply enough for Aline to go on giving them a chance to put out to sea again and a haven.

Ah, if only those days had never existed!

"That kid, he's a positive pest! Oh, you can pride yourself on having foisted a nice job on me! If I had to have *that* hanging round my skirts for a whole year, I'd go out of my mind or into a nunnery . . . That little brat never lets up for a moment, he goes on and on till he drives you crazy with his revolution and his trade-unions, his ships, Madagascar, his father, his father's good looks, his father's bravery, his father's old house, his father's return . . . Don't you sometimes wonder if he isn't a bit cracked?"

I replied that André had a thousand excuses. I did not revolt against Aline. I did not hate Aline.

"Not right in the head, the son of a drunk, and what's more, a spoiled little brat with no feelings! If it wasn't

146

that he was useful to us, I'd send him packing. Do you hear me? Throw him out, like a dirty dog! Even his way of behaving is nasty and underhanded. You never know if he's fond of you or only puts up with you or, even, if he hates you. A good hiding now and then would do him no end of good. At least it might turn him into something resembling a child!"

I kept silent. Indignation and rage were welling up inside me. But they must have been very feeble since I succeeded in mastering them. And they did not dim the delight Aline gave me.

I kept silent.

"I'm sure he spies on us when we're making love, or at any rate that he *has* done it. I bet he knows perfectly well what we do and how we do it. He's got a vicious look when he stares at me, haven't you ever noticed it? He doesn't stare at me frankly, oh no, he stares at my bosom—when I'm wearing a low-necked dress. Those sharp little eyes are much too bright. Why? Are you going to invent another excuse for him? Vice starts early and when it starts there's no stopping it in these children of alcoholics! He's a dirty-minded little beast and I find it hard not to slap him at times, I can tell you. One day that's going to happen, I warn you . . ."

I kept silent. I kept silent.

The shrill monologue sometimes broke out vehemently again under the myrobalan trees before the rain. Always before the rain, on the threshold of the rain. I wonder why.

147

"This time, it's really too much. I can't stand the sight of him any more. I shall end by having hysterics or doing something foolish. Even my husband's noticed the change in me. 'What's the matter, Aline? You aren't well, darling. You fly into black rages over nothing or else you're even gloomier than Madame Galantie.' Obviously I didn't tell him it was because of that sniveling brat who's stupider and more of a nuisance than ten other kids of his age. But I feel I've come to the end of my tether. Perhaps it amuses you—you've got your own reasons—to go on endlessly embroidering the legend of his father, and his precious father going to do this, that and the other, an entire afternoon. But it doesn't amuse *me* in the least. Honestly, not in the very least! I'm fed to the teeth with it! I honestly believe I hate him! . . . He ought to be put in a reformatory, if you want my opinion! It's all he deserves."

She pulled herself up, and that was even more horrible.

"Goodness, how naughty of me to let myself go like that! Forgive me. It was very wrong of me. After all, he's our little Cupid's torch, isn't he?"

How could I be so obstinately determined not to break with her? Ah, I was bound hand and foot. She held me by my senses—and by my jealousy. The man who had replaced me on the charity Committee, which she continued to attend every Saturday, in her gray suit, had made it clearly understood, she told me that . . . well . . . He had even tried to kiss her and to fix a rendezvous with her.

"He's not bad looking at all . . . He's got quite nice manners, and pretty hands . . ."

148

"You wouldn't have anything to do with that man, Aline?"

"No, of course not, but . . ."

"I might kill you! Mark what I say, I'm not talking lightly. I might kill you."

"You won't kill me, I know that. But I shan't do it, all the same. For quite other reasons."

Was it true that André had spied on us one day when we thought he was tranquilly lying on the chaise longue on the terrace? Did she imagine it? Was she consciously lying? It seemed to me that little by little he was drawing away from me. That nowadays I aroused in him a kind of fear or repugnance.

XVI

As if by design Louis Galantie had chosen this particular period to pay frequent visits to my uncle. He came practically every Sunday, with his smart blue-gray felt hat and his cigar. He is the only man I have truly and consistently loathed and of whom I still think with hatred.

Like Fernand Joliet, he was one of my cousins. Fortune had favored him. He was witty and well-informed rather than intelligent but he had steered his course cleverly. His position—secretary-general in line to become one of the three directors of Jackson Brothers Ltd., our biggest sugar exporters—made him a star-personality in the family, hardly less envied than Emile Galantie. The latter, keenly susceptible to a polish he himself did not possess, a cart-

horse confronted with a racehorse, took pleasure in re-
ceiving him and held him in particular esteem. Louis's
vivacious talk, his jokes and his puns, enchanted him. I
think he took pride, as the head of this vast family of
nephews and nieces, most of whom had disappointed him,
in seeing him so highly placed and destined to rise higher
still. It compensated him for his mortifying failures.

Moreover, my cousin was thrifty, though he cultivated
the appearance of a lavish, pleasure-loving aristocrat, which
was highly useful to his career and increased what he called
his glamour. Added to his other qualities, it widened his
sphere of contacts. In the hands of the secretary-general
of Jackson Brothers Ltd., money was safe in a solid fortress.
Emile Galantie could not but have felt attracted to such a
man. He had given concrete proof of it. Two years earlier,
when he had entertained grave fears about his health
(there had been talk of cancer of the intestines), he had
made Louis's eldest son who was said to be following hard
in his father's footsteps, his principal heir. Besides the
house, nearly three quarters of his property, including his
lime-kilns and the numerous shares he held in various
sugar-refineries, would go to the youth, Louis administer-
ing the estate till his son came of age . . .

Had my cousin become anxious about his interests since
little André had come to live with us? Yes. I had already
realized it from certain allusions, as well as from a certain
nervousness in his manner. One would have had to be the
least perspicacious of men not to notice it. Those allusions,

usually of the meanest kind, concerning the unpromising future of a child with such heredity and such bad example, amazed me. Could a man of that stamp sink so low? But doubtless he told himself that a childless old man who had always longed for a child might very likely let himself yield to some belated sentimental impulse. André, in his eyes, had become a possible heir. From now on he was engaged in a remorseless battle. He had promised himself he would win it.

In the early days, his attack had been discreet; he was biding his time. It was a matter of gloomy remarks about the hardness of the times, of innuendoes, of passing clouds of depression, of sudden flares of enthusiasm when he spoke of his son. He talked of the frenzied and fruitful studies of Jacques who wanted to become an engineer and the grandiose projects he entertained on his behalf—on condition, of course, that young Jacques disposed of a comfortable basic sum to build on when he reached man's estate. In sentences whose meaning was clear, if not stated in so many words, he was asking Uncle Emile to respect his original intentions and what would be even better, to give him a new and solemn assurance.

"You know," Emile Galantie sometimes said to me in the office in the rue Mahé which was usually the scene of his confidences, "I ought to despise Louis. That would be a normal reaction. But somehow, I can't. On the contrary, I only feel all the more violently drawn to him."

He would stress his remark by nodding his head and

152

fidgeting with his watch chain. Then he would watch a cart or a motor go by before turning back to me.

"You don't quite follow me, do you? In my place you'd be exasperated if you knew someone was running after you for a legacy and simply and solely for that. You'd promptly remake your will and cut him out of it without the slightest scruple . . ."

"That's to say . . . If you don't mind, I'll refrain from judging Louis Galantie."

"I'm going to put a question to you. Heaven knows I'm fond of you. I told you so once: you resemble me in my youth and nothing can be dearer to an old man's heart. I've patiently educated you so that you should be my perfect successor in this practice, another me. In short, you've become my shadow, just as one day you'll acquire a shadow who will replace you . . . Would I have acted like this if you had been not only unworthy of my confidence but a mere mediocrity, with only middling cards in your hand?"

"Yes, I think you would."

"As a proof of the friendship between us?"

"That counts. You know that as well as I do!"

"Then you're wrong . . . Because I shouldn't have done it. It would have wrung my heart, but I wouldn't have done it. I would have asked you to leave your desk and your files to someone else, even if he were as indifferent to me as any Tom, Dick, or Harry. When you've put your heart into a life-work—whether it's a question of a profession, or, since we're talking of Louis, of wealth acquired penny by penny, by effort after effort, bold stroke after bold stroke—you don't easily resign yourself to seeing it mutilated. You'll realize that full well, later on, most certainly when you're my age—I am not fond of Louis. No. He means nothing to me. Often he irritates, if not infuriates me. For example, doesn't he try, when we're in company—especially in the company of important people—to lord it over me with his glibness and gift of gab or his wit? I'm neither blind nor deaf. As a man, I've no patience with him. But as a public figure—I suppose one can call him that!—and as a financier, I respect him. And his son Jacques will be just like him, I realized that at once. My lime-kilns, my shares, my various other bits of property will be guaranteed not to go up in smoke. They're part of me, I repeat, I've put my life-blood into them . . ."

His usually moist blue gaze became, as it were, metallic. Not hard, but imbued with this tremendous will to endure. "Louis is extremely worried about the presence of little André in my home. That's obvious to the meanest intelligence. He thinks—with some semblance of reason—that heir for heir, child for child, all I need is my pot of violet ink, my pen, and a sheet of paper to substitute one André Joliet for one Jacques Galantie. Why the devil doesn't he use his head? His behavior surprises and disappoints me, though I take off my hat to his desperate eagerness which is certainly worthy of the picture I've formed of him. What mental aberration, with unpardonable ignorance of my character, could make him even imagine I might leave An-

154

dré a fortune which his father would lose no time in dissipating, if not drinking away?"

That particular day, I leaped to my feet in one bound. My face must have been crimson.

"Whatever you leave to André, I swear to administer it personally. It would be easy for you to insert that clause in any will . . ."

Slowly, he turned his back on me and pressed his forehead against the window pane. I was no longer there; I no longer counted . . . I urged my point.

"That boy starts off in life with a terrible handicap. Your help—a gesture from you—a smile from you beyond the grave—could save him. It's your plain duty. I ask you, I implore you to . . ."

He interrupted me. He went on imperturbably watching what was going on in the street.

"Two things will always prevent me from granting your prayer. Fernand could make a stone pity him: he wouldn't have to be much of a magician to get you interested in his lot, however hard-boiled you meant to be about him. Besides which, he's done me too much harm! He's humiliated me in every possible way. He's shamed my honor, my affection, my very blood. He squeezed me like a sponge before he obliged me to go and grovel to a magistrate to prevent his going to prison . . ."

His mouth was bitter. He seemed all at once to have no teeth, his lips drooped in two long folds at the corners like the mouth of a tortoise. He looked at his watch. It was a mannerism of his, to show me he did not wish to pursue this conversation.

"No, never," he went on. "However sorry I may be for your pupil, I shall never give him more than I am giving him now. I would gladly tell Louis he's letting his imagination run wild but I fear he'd feel obliged to pretend to be disinterested and then I shouldn't be able to resist being sarcastic to him. It's not worth the trouble. And besides," (he gave his harsh laugh) "perhaps it gives me satisfaction to see him crawling to me. It's some compensation for being outshone. The star adoring the old toad—don't you find that an edifying spectacle? Something Virgilian about it, don't you think? . . ."

It is possible that Louis Galantie's anxieties coincided with a difficult phase in his life or in his business affairs, or even with some passing worry about his health. No one but himself could have told us if this was so and I was the last person to try and find any mitigating circumstances for him. His character changed from Sunday to Sunday. At the moment he was positively miserly. The malicious pleasure my uncle took in encouraging him to cut down his expenses no doubt played a large part in the degradation that was taking place before my eyes. Louis was not unaware of the irony that lit up that old face. Did he read something else in it, the threat that seemed more obvious every time, of that substitution of heirs that he feared? He

156

THE *Isle*

had become extraordinarily soured. His customary pleas-
antries had given place to ill-natured backbiting. He was
trying to forget his torment by slandering other people, no
matter who, whether they were members of the family or
not.

He would gladly have done the same about me—for he
knew my attachment to André and certainly held me responsible for what he feared might happen—but he refrained. Perhaps he wanted to humor me? He believed I
had great influence with our uncle. Besides, what could he
have told about me? Stories of my sex-life that were beginning to get abroad? He was a man who would not balk
at employing the methods of a policeman to obtain information about me. However, he still had enough wit to
realize that Emile would have jeered at him. He was interested only in my legal capacities . . .

He insulted Aunt Marthe on the slightest provocation.
Clumsily, though he was usually so subtle. Did he hope to
worm his way back into Emile's favor? The long, dry,
wrinkled face remained impenetrable. At certain moments
I had to restrain myself from bursting out laughing.

I observed him, I admit, with cruel satisfaction. He had
grown thinner and I rejoiced in the fact. There were dark
shadows under his small, pig-like eyes. But the voice remained warm and vibrant. He bemoaned the anarchy that
was rife everywhere and the shame that menaced our family since one of us, Fernand, might be confused in decent
people's minds with those black agitators who desired

157

nothing but loot. These were Emile Galantie's own sentiments, but the latter said nothing, or even, if it suited his mood, he would find some excuse for his "prodigal nephew" while disapproving of his political activities. "Ah yes, Uncle? You're too generous! Personally, I condemn him out of hand. And besides . . ." And besides there remained the affair of the forged signature. The sad, deplorable, hateful affair of the forgery!

"There are people I don't dare go to see any more. I always have the feeling they're going to ask me: 'And how about your cousin, Joliet? Will he get out of it, in your opinion? You must admit it's a lamentable business and all the whites are going to get dirty names as a result.' They have the politeness not to say it, but they think it all the same . . ."

Or, another occasion:

"Misfortune has good results, sometimes, Uncle. You're shocked by Fernand's intemperance." (Yet Emile Galantie had not so much as breathed a word on the subject.) "Like everyone else on this island, I like my six o'clock whiskey and soda. Well, I've given it up and for good. No doubt Fernand began without thinking any harm would come of a little daily apéritif. But the habit quickly got a hold on him—and one's seen the result . . ."

"He's had a great many misfortunes," said my uncle with a wry, forced smile. "That doesn't blot out his faults, admittedly. But, to a certain extent, the past explains the present."

158

"Do you think so?"

There was a spiteful gleam in the depths of the small pig-like gray eyes.

"A man can never be forgiven for wallowing in the mud . . . You'll contradict me by referring to heredity. Granted. Charles Joliet drank too much too. Let's say Fernand is less responsible than others but he remains largely to blame. Just as his son will also be a drinker by heredity and also to blame for having given in to the vice."

"Oh," said Emile Galantie in honeyed tones, "don't be alarmed. I'm not pretending that Fernand's a saint, far from it. Still . . ."

The "still" hovered disturbingly in the air, like a bell sounding in the fog, a passing-bell tolling from a haunted steeple.

For two successive Sundays Louis arrived accompanied by his wife and his three children, the infantry of the siege. Irène, his wife, was kind-hearted. We were told how charitable and willing to help she was, and some very fine acts of hers during the recent cyclones were cited. I felt she was embarrassed by her premature stoutness which she pretended to laugh at; she tried to take up as little room as possible (oh Lord, her predilection for that little rocking chair which barely contained her!) and she did not realize the absurdity of her situation. Pious enough to crack the vaults of a cathedral. Not insignificant, but as if in a trance . . . Jacques, the infant prodigy, the first-born of the litter, acting no doubt on his father's recommendations, settled the hash of mathematics, Latin, ancient history, etc. like a verbal mincing-machine that started grinding again at the slightest question. Living as I did in such intimacy with my uncle, I knew that he was greatly impressed, but he had decided not to show any sign of this. He would continue implacably to keep up this farce of indifference. Was it inhuman of him? I was, I still am, too much a party to the whole affair to venture an opinion.

I was not at all keen that André should be involved with Louis's children. They would be nasty to him if I did not watch out; they had been so much indoctrinated that they would regard him much as a dog who has to be chased out of the room if one wants to eat in peace. I entrusted him to Aline. For there was no question of my absenting myself: Emile Galantie would have held it against me if I had not assisted at the Sunday Louis-baiting, he needed his spectator. I was certain that Aline—whatever her mood— would not go as far as to depict his father to him as a drunkard and a thief. For that was precisely what I was afraid of at home. That one of the little Galanties or Louis in person would throw that in his face, the children because they had heard it said only too often and had learned to detest the intruder and Louis out of brutal vengeance on the boy, who in his eyes, had despoiled him. I guessed he was capable of it. I *knew* he was capable of it.

I asked my uncle from time to time: "Do you still think he deserves your esteem?"

"More than ever. He's the kind of shark who could depopulate the ocean all on his own."

"Admit that if Fernand's a wet rag, this fellow isn't any better . . . I'm not sure he isn't worse . . . I'm going to use a word that will shock you: I call Louis a scoundrel."

"All right, he is! Do you think I care? A wet rag can't do anything without tearing itself to shreds. A swine of Louis's kind makes whatever you put in his hands fructify. He's a born financier. He isn't overcome with shyness and pious scruples when it comes to dealing with money."

Alas, I had to confess I was wrong: he was baring the depths of his soul to me. And he did not seem to understand my astonishment . . .

"You know this man only comes to your house because he's reckoning you must die soon. Yet that doesn't put your back up—doesn't give you an irresistible desire to give him a good kick somewhere where it hurts? Admit that's somewhat unusual!"

He made a calm, slow gesture.

"You're basing all your arguments on sentiment, that's your mistake. *Sentiment* plays no part, nor do I intend it to, in anything concerning my inheritance. Sentiment has not counted for much in my life. Once again, that's the fault of your aunt but we'll skip that . . . I am leaving my fortune to Jacques Galantie, therefore to Louis, because my fortune is like a living being to me that must go on living after my death so that I can go on living through it. That's all. I've already explained how I feel on this subject. I will add, if that will satisfy you, that I have lived outside my heart, if I can put it like that, away from my heart and even without my heart, that my heart has always represented my poverty which I hate, that Marthe has never allowed me to make anything whatsoever blossom in it. I don't have to go and find the spring of my actions in a desert . . ."

"In that case tell Louis once and for all he can sleep soundly on his pillow. He makes me sick . . ."

"How exacting you are, my dear boy! Won't you leave me my theater? I'm attached to it. I haven't had much opportunity of amusing myself, any more than I've had much opportunity of loving."

XVII

I shall never forget that Saturday. What demon sent Louis Galantie to Grand-Bourg on a Saturday rather than a Sunday? He had not visited us for over a month.

The weather was what the old colored people called "tufted"; everywhere there was a mass of fine white clouds, faintly edged with coppery-brown, drawn out thinner toward the zenith—the sign of southwest wind and the first chill of winter. It was my birthday. I do not know how Aline had managed it but she had persuaded her husband to spend the day from early dawn with his former chief mate. This man, a mulatto, was a rather odd character. He was affirmed by some people to be an ascetic, by others to be half-crazy. He lived up on the mountain where he bred fighting-cocks, but he relied mainly on the charity of his friends for his subsistence. He had married the widow of one of his brothers and she had given him a daughter, a tall, gawky, short-sighted girl whom he adored. He was said to have retired to the plateau so as to be as far as possible from the sea and to regret it less. Indeed he could not even hear the sea mentioned without promptly flying into a rage. He positively worshipped Bruckner, wrote to him on all the great feast days, and more than once, the Captain had discreetly helped him.

My mistress was waiting for me. We were to be alone with each other for a whole day. We would even be able to have lunch together.

"And I've secretly had a bottle of claret sent up and hidden it. It costs a fortune, you know!"

"You're completely mad! . . . To go to such expense for me!"

"No, no. Nothing could be good enough for this Saturday. I've also thought of a salad of palm-hearts . . . you adore that."

"For goodness' sake, don't bother, Aline! It's the pleasure of being with you that matters. The rest isn't worth thinking about and the cyclones have made everything fantastically expensive . . ."

I could not make her listen to reason. She was determined that this should be "the most marvelous day in the world." I myself had bought her a bracelet which I thought very pretty though it was little more than costume jewelry.

164

"Above all, no André, promise me that? Whatever happens . . . This Saturday must be ours and ours only."

She shook out her soft mane of black scented hair. She was smiling. She was once again the Aline of the first days of our liaison. It was true that lately she had been very much on edge and almost cantankerous, even to me . . . Now she was radiant.

"A day to live to the very marrow of our bones, you understand? A day among days—for how do we know there'll ever come another one like it? So many obstacles could arise! We'll make love to each other as if it were the very first time. We won't be just lover and mistress: this will be something else—I don't know what—that will keep us always together even if we have to be separated afterward . . ."

I had neglected her a good deal during the past month, especially since the only too visible change in André where I was concerned. I avoided going out. We had seen each other only three times. Oh, I was in no doubt that I should relapse! But I had been honestly trying to win back my boy's heart. She had sworn to herself that this birthday of mine was to reconcile us, assuring me that henceforth she would be more patient and understanding, and I put up no resistance . . . I told André, as well as Marthe and Emile Galantie, that I was going over to the Plaine-des-Cafres on business, by the 8:25 train.

I had hardly left the house when I met Louis. He had been ill, as I had supposed. "Oh nothing, just a bit run-down after influenza!" His imposing façade had crumbled away. He was pale and he had cut his chin deeply while shaving; he looked altogether unlike his usual immaculately groomed self. His entire person seemed to have sagged and collapsed. He saw me and straightened himself up. Defiantly? Not so much that, it seemed to me, as in an attempt to recover his swagger. We shook hands tepidly.

"I'm sorry I shan't have the pleasure of your company, Louis. I've been called over to the Plaine-des-Cafres."

"Oh, have you?"

"Yes. I'll try not to be back too late. You'll be taking the last train, as usual?"

"Probably."

My heart contracted. If it had been feasible, I would have retraced my steps. Here was danger threatening on every side. I felt feverish. But I cannot break my word to you, Aline, can I? Ever since this morning, ever since yesterday, I have never stopped thinking of this whole day with you. We have never had such a thing. We have had to steal time in little snatches and today there will be no haggling over the hours . . . All the same, Aline, if I had only known! If I had only been able to foresee this! I am sure some vile plot is being hatched . . .

Wasn't Louis walking much faster? Hadn't he regained the elasticity of his step? He was no longer the man who had shuffled slowly forward to greet me and had looked ten years older. Had he decided at last to speak straight out to my uncle and did he think it would be less difficult for him in my absence? Or was he furious with resentment and André would pay the price of it? That was it, for certain! And Emile Galantie, busy with his game of teasing a dog with a lump of sugar, would let him go to any length of ignominy . . . I wanted to run after him, and shout: "You needn't have the slightest anxiety about that will, I give you my word. Our uncle won't leave André anything, he's told me so over and over again. For pity's sake, don't destroy that child! Be respectful about his father in front of him. The reverse would have tragic consequences. I've moved heaven and earth up to now to spare him the shock. Help me . . ." A foolish pride restrained me. The fear of my uncle played a large part in it. I stopped still in my tracks. I watched his figure receding. I cursed and cursed chance for letting this happen . . .

Even after Aline, in her very low-cut blouse, had welcomed me so warmly, even in those moments when it becomes easy to believe in eternal bliss, I still kept thinking of Louis Galantie. Why, when he left me, was he wearing that resolute expression? Resolute—and satisfied.

"Is it only my fancy, Aline darling? I'm frightened . . . I'm afraid he won't be able to restrain himself, that his rage will drive him to do anything, no matter what. He's like an animal that's going to bite. An animal that thinks it's been frustrated and bites its master's shadow because it daren't bite the master himself."

"Forget all about it! You're spoiling everything . . . Forget it, I tell you."

"I've got responsibilities toward this child. I'm the in-
dispensable buffer between him and life. And just today,
when he'll need me so much!"

She sighed. Her naked breasts, her belly, summoned me;
I could hear my own blood pulsing in her veins.

"If I meant a little to you, you'd rise above your worries.
I give you everything."

"You do mean something to me and you know it. You
mean more than anyone . . . That's the terrible thing."

"Terrible?"

"It's love too, Aline. Yes, love . . ."

"Don't think of anything but me! Now is the moment
. . . the moment I've waited for . . ."

It was when passion had shattered me that the image of
Louis vanished from my mind. The image of André little
by little faded away too, like a quivering mist dissolving
above the dew. A sudden gust of wind, and then nothing.
And then the singing of the blood in every vein of my
deeply satisfied flesh. Aline, shattered like myself, still
burning against the whole length of my body . . . And
afterward, more . . .

XVIII

I returned home about eight and I knew at once that my apprehensions of the morning had unfortunately not been idle. My uncle greeted me with extreme coldness. He had certainly made a great effort to control himself at the sight of me but he was still in an inner turmoil.

"Louis is reassured now . . ."

"Ah, so you've at last followed my advice?" I mumbled.

He growled something I did not catch. This admission to Louis Galantie dumbfounded me. It was so inconsistent with his obstinacy! Hadn't he declared only the other day that he was going to enjoy the amusing situation to the end? What incident had been crucial enough to make him change his point of view? From his surly embarrassment

I guessed what had decided him. My cousin had descended to infamy and he had not prevented him from doing so, not out of sadism but to prove to himself that his will could not be deflected by any contingency. Afterward, he had been ashamed; he had realized that he himself was behaving just as monstrously. He had tried to put the brake on for the sake of the future . . .

"Louis was more than grotesque . . . If you'd deigned to be present instead of going off on your affairs, incidentally I don't know which ones, this regrettable scene would not have taken place."

He did not look at me. He had taken out his handkerchief and was nervously wiping his hands.

"It was the same thing the night your pupil fell ill. You were miles away when you ought to have been here. Anyone would think you had a flair for catastrophes . . ."

"Stop preaching at me," I interrupted. "What has happened?"

He turned his back on me. He was monumentally silent.

"What has happened?" I repeated, placing myself in front of him again. "What has Louis done? I met him this morning on my way to the station. He seemed to me a little odd. That made me suspect he might be going to make a scene."

"This had to happen," he growled. "If it hadn't been Louis, someone else would have done the job, tomorrow or the next day or some time. It was no use your keeping that child in cotton-wool, the truth was bound to come out.

How could you have protected him from it? By putting him to sleep for the rest of his days?"

"What? Louis dared . . .?"

"You must realize that I didn't have time to intervene," Emile Galantie said harshly.

He could not forgive me for not having been there. All the reproaches he might logically have addressed to himself, he flung back at me. *I* was the guilty one.

"No, I didn't have time to intervene," he told me again, in a still harsher voice.

He rebelled.

"I'm not anybody's guardian! I've had my bellyful of this tragi-comedy! . . . You only had to give up your outing and play the part of a faithful watchdog since you thought it necessary. Weren't you expecting this incident? Yes! You knew it was in the air. There's no excuse for you . . ."

"What did Louis Galantie do?" I asked after a moment. "You haven't answered me."

"He lost his temper . . ."

There was a brief silence, then he resumed: "Yes, all of a sudden. Because André asked him, I can't remember in what connection, if he knew Madagascar and if he thought his father would come back from there soon. You know how boring that kid can be at times. He gets on *your* nerves sometimes . . ."

He took a few steps toward the veranda which looked

171

out on the sea. That calm sea which might perhaps comfort him with its tranquillity.

"What were you trying to say? Most of the damage was already done. I swear to God, there was nothing I could do about it. All I could do was to calm Louis down and beg him to watch his words in the future. I did that, though it cost me a great deal."

He added defiantly: "I hasten to assure you that my intentions concerning Louis Galantie have not changed one iota."

"I don't care! To hell with your damned legacy! Give your filthy money to anyone you like . . ."

He trembled at the insult. For a second, his mouth remained open without a sound issuing from it. His neck seemed thinner and more shrunken than usual, under a network of hard veins. The Adam's apple protruded strangely.

"Forgive me," I murmured. "You've set my mind in such a whirl."

I went up to him. He had to get me out of this hole of icy water. I put my hand on his shoulder. It was a gesture I had never made before.

"I implore you, stand by me! I don't know what's in the wind, what's going to happen next. I would never have thought Louis would lose his head like that. I was a little afraid of his reactions, I admit. But I persuaded myself that at least he'd preserve his self-respect and have some semblance of charity for that boy, even if only because he had children himself . . . What did he say to André?"

"Everything," muttered my uncle, disengaging himself.

"That Fernand was a drunkard?"

"Yes."

"And . . . the affair?"

"Yes, that too."

"The rest?"

"All the rest . . . For goodness' sake, shut up, will you?"

He grabbed up a chair and put it down again violently.

"You always work things up into tragedies," he went on. "Wait and see what happens before getting in a panic. Your pupil obviously doesn't believe this . . . this ill-natured gossip. Otherwise he probably wouldn't have consented to eat his dinner."

He stopped fidgeting with the chair, opened the glass door and walked out. He took a few paces toward the sea, making for the landing-stage which would soon be almost submerged by the tide.

"I was the one who had no dinner. I couldn't face it."

I had followed him. He turned round in a single movement, as if his body were all of a piece.

"Will you all go to hell and stop bothering me with your problems? with childhood and its sorrows and disappointments? I haven't had a child, these things are none of my concern. You'd better understand that once and for all and not be so insistent on making my few remaining years a burden. I don't want to have to keep incessantly searching my heart as you seem to think you have the right to oblige me to. Enough of all this! Don't bother any more

173

about my heart and don't hope any more from it either. For five months since this brat has been under my roof, there hasn't been a moment's quiet in my home. And I need quiet, if only for the sake of my health. Call it silence, if you prefer . . ."

He drew an envelope out of his pocket.

"I've just written to Louis, who went off by the three o'clock train, probably in order to avoid you. I've asked him to stop coming here for a while, till things have shaken down."

An angry sea was surging inside me, buffeting me with sand and water, dying down then bursting out again. Aline, Louis, André. Then again, Aline, Louis Galantie, André. That stormy Saturday ought never to have dawned. What was I going to do now? How could I heal, how repair the ravages? What words could I use? When the luminous buoy is extinguished, the sea is only a swirling flood, black as midnight.

Emile Galantie was waiting. Was I going to propose a solution? I remained silent. I was in a prison. The entire world was my jailer.

"I can only see one way out," I said with an effort. "André must have a radical upheaval. Doctor Malleret is right and we've hesitated too long. The only thing that can save him now is that boarding school."

He flung up his arms.

"Always paying out! Emile Galantie isn't a man, oh no; he's the family purse! Clean hands, dirty hands, they all

174

dig into it at will. Not so much as a by-your-leave or a thank-you! Why worry?"

"And, according to you, boarding school is the panacea?" he went on, after a moment.

"It would plunge him straight away into an entirely different setting," I said, "and believe me I'd be the first to suffer at the thought of his going to Gros-Bois. It would separate him from us, and perhaps from everything else too. André would learn to live; to begin with he would have companions of his own age . . ."

"Who'd finish off Louis's work for him? Who'd drive that cruel nail in deeper and deeper, provided it *can* be driven in any deeper?"

"Not children, Uncle! That's idiotic! Children wouldn't do that . . ."

"Children have parents. Don't forget Fernand Joliet isn't only a drunkard; his attempts to stir up trouble have set everyone against him. I realized that only too well a little while ago when I wanted the charge against him to be quashed. They did it for me, not for him . . . How do we even know if the Fathers will accept this tainted child? I'm by no means sure of it. They've always been exceedingly careful not to offend their clients' susceptibilities. Tell me, for example, if you know of *one* little black boy or even one mulatto at St. Joseph's, Gros-Bois. I regret only one thing: when I packed Fernand off, I ought to have packed his son off with him too. It was positively insane of me to take him in here. I shall be accused of having done

175

so out of miserliness, but it was something entirely different that decided me."

He was speaking in a weary, monotonous voice, in strange contrast to his raging of a few moments ago. He had folded his arms. His face was still turned toward the sea.

"He's an unfortunate little shipwrecked creature who will never be able to live like other children, no matter where he goes. Honestly, I don't think he's intelligent . . . don't get your back up! He doesn't even know how to accept existence with a modicum of sensuality, like an animal. A tiny little cloudy brain, and furthermore, a deranged one. He mills eternally over that *idée fixe* of his and can't take in anything else. And everywhere and always he'll be harshly treated, crucified. Fernand behaved like a criminal the day he took to drink. He's done something more criminal still by stuffing André's head with ideas that won't hold water, that bear no relation to reality and that can only drive people to treat him cruelly. If even it were all based on some semblance of truth! But Fernand's only a feeble, contemptible chap and everyone knows it. Taking revenge on him is so easy—so tempting . . ."

He was staring at the water, at the big coral reef to the left of the harbor wall, that the sea had now covered over again. He said, without raising his eyes:

"You've been off after a woman, haven't you, all this miserable day? Do you think I was taken in? That was your business at Plaine-des-Cafres."

I had blushed to the ears. Did he notice it? He went on

176

pretending to be interested in nothing but the rising tide.

"I rather think it's nearer home, at Madame Bruckner's, we ought to have looked for you," he let fall, as if casually.

"Excuse me," I muttered. "That's no one's business but mine."

"Rubbish!"

He had reached the end of the little jetty and was now retracing his steps.

"Personally, I don't give a damn. I haven't the least desire to turn you into a monk and I prefer a liaison of this kind to your chasing after the type of women who end up by ruining you. But have the goodness to see there's no scandal! I've had enough of this game of mending broken pots. I won't stand it. It's good for youth to indulge its fiery passions. So blaze away as much as you like, but preserve other people from the sparks. That's the condition I impose on you, as long as I'm alive and you're under my roof . . . Nevertheless, you might have abstained from this nonsense today, you couldn't have chosen a worse moment."

I stood glued to the stones of that jetty. My skin stung with salt and iodine. I cursed the blush that crimsoned my face.

"Let's go in," said my uncle, after he had sufficiently enjoyed the spectacle. "The chill's coming on. You won't like it a bit when you're my age."

He took my arm. Was he trying to get me to forgive him? Human, at last! Almost fatherly.

"I mentioned the name of Madame Bruckner so that you

should know Emile Galantie keeps his eyes open. It's a good idea to remember that occasionally . . . Let's drop the subject! And don't go and worry yourself sick over it! I'm perfectly aware that life here isn't amusing for a boy of twenty-eight. I shan't disapprove of you as long as you and your mistress keep up appearances as regards Bruckner and any other people we know. As to your son, as you call him . . ."

He hesitated. His hand gripped my arm harder, more urgently.

"Try to surmount this obstacle, to wipe out the effect of Louis's unfortunate words. You alone hold the key to success or failure. André trusts you. He loves you. You're the one person who could do it. But, alas, he'll always be heavily handicapped. That child is inexorably doomed—unless you can manage to harden him sufficiently to overcome his misfortune. That's what your job is. Not to commiserate, but to harden. You've got to realize that. You're not dealing with a normal child. Sheer stupidity, going blindly by what Malleret says, as you're doing! André doesn't need coddling, he needs to become a different person. As things have been going up to now, it was partly yourself you loved in him. I've been frightened of that—it was your foretaste of fatherhood. Take care. For the sake of your own heart, take care. You don't know what the future has in store for you . . ."

We went indoors again—just as I came indoors again just now on account of the same chill that was falling

178

and almost at the same pace as then. Is it Emile Galantie's voice in the wind that is soughing more and more
sadly? "A tainted little creature who will never be able
to live like any other boy. Honestly I don't think he's intelligent. He doesn't even know how to accept life with
the sensuality of an animal . . ." To my mind, that life ran
its brief course like a miniature version of the Passion.
Who then was Judas and who Caiaphas and who Pilate?
Who was John, the loving? Bruckner? Captain Bruckner,
if there is an after-life, if there is a heaven, if there is a
judgment, do not stand witness against Aline and me!

XIX

For a few weeks, I was able to hope that the incident had not hurt him too cruelly and that I should succeed in making him get over it, thanks to Captain Bruckner. On the evening of the Monday after that Saturday he had turned up at the usual time for whist bearing a large, odd-looking square basket. He had an awkward, embarrassed air.

"Well, my dear Bruckner, whatever are you bringing us, arriving like Father Christmas? Do you want us to give three guesses? I give up in advance. Let me off!"

"A cock, Monsieur Galantie. I hope you don't mind?"

"A cock?"

My uncle was first surprised, then suspicious he was being made fun of, but he ended by bursting out laughing.

It was so totally unexpected! Bruckner's air of confusion added a note of burlesque to the scene.

"Why on earth a cock? Dead and plucked, I hope. Have you ever heard me express any desire to go in for poultry-raising in all the twenty years you've known me?"

"It's for your great-nephew. A fighting-cock—a very fine Indian cock I've been given by my ex-mate, Ludovic Snarle—I've already mentioned him to you . . ."

Up to now he had remained on his guard. Now he was beaming.

"Apparently it's a bird of the best breed. Obviously I'm far from being an expert in these matters, but Snarle assures me it is and I've no reason to doubt his word. I thought that by organizing cock-fights for André and putting up his champion against the ones in the neighborhood . . ."

"You're mad!" said my uncle.

He surveyed the Captain contemptuously with his cold eyes. Bruckner could not sustain the gaze. He had relapsed into his original embarrassment. He put his basket down at his feet.

"How could such an absurd, preposterous notion have got into your head? I'm sorry, but really . . ."

"You see, Monsieur Galantie," said Bruckner, after a moment, "it occurred to me that this might be an excellent way of distracting the child from his loneliness or his depression. That it would give him some excitement, some chance of having the little thrills natural to his age that he's missing so much. I'd make it my personal business to arrange the contests—that goes without saying. Boys have always been very fond of these cock-fights. Mine were crazy about them in the old days."

He gave the basket a tentative kick and the cock clucked *sotto voce.*

"Yes, that was my idea. I thought André would be delighted, above all that it would occupy his mind. Give him an interest in life, let's say . . . Don't worry, I haven't breathed a word to him of my purchase."

"So, on top of everything, it's a purchase?"

"Forget it, forget it," said the Captain eagerly. "My friend Ludovic's always hard up from one year's end to the other and this was just one way of helping him a bit . . . I'll take my basket back home. I'll easily find some way of getting rid of this unfortunate fowl . . ."

"Oh, all right," grumbled my uncle, even more annoyed than he allowed it to appear, "since the thing's done! . . . But you might have consulted me beforehand."

"Oh, the whole thing came about by pure chance! I assure you I didn't go to Plateau Pitot with any such plan in my mind . . ."

His smile was disarming. There was an almost childish radiance in his thin, thoughtful face.

"It was over there the opportunity presented itself. I started thinking about the idea and then . . . The cock's a magnificent one, as you'll see. A really fine specimen."

"Call André," Emile Galantie said to me curtly.

182

He avoided Bruckner's satisfied gaze, obviously to keep his temper in check. So did I. I was already one of those neurotics who cannot endure the unexpected and whose minds are only easy when nothing disturbs their humdrum daily routine. A cock! What senile imbecility! It went without saying that I would have to build a pen for it. To whom else could the task be entrusted? And I loathed everything to do with hammer and nails, wire-netting, and all the rest! No one could be clumsier at any form of manual labor! Captain Bruckner certainly had not considered this business from any point of view but his own.

"Call André," my uncle repeated louder, casting a glance of involuntary disgust at the basket.

"How cantankerous you look, dear!" said Marthe. "Anyone would think you lived on maize and that this poor cock was going to squabble with you over your share of it!"

She smiled at Bruckner who did not dare smile back at her.

"Shut up, will you!" exclaimed Emile Galantie. "I'm the master here."

"Don't worry, nobody doubts it. One's only got to look at the life we lead here to know who runs the place . . . You're thinking you'll have to buy netting and stakes and corrugated iron and your generous heart bleeds at the thought. Isn't that so?"

"Mind your own business."

"I . . . I'll bring everything that's necessary over tomorrow," put in Bruckner hastily.

183

Why did I feel such a spurt of rage? Was I still jealous of him? Jealous of the old Captain of the wonderful stories? In spite of the thunderclap of the day before yesterday?

"*I* shall do the paying."

"Certainly not. I intended all along . . ."

"For goodness' sake, stop arguing!" I said with a fury I could not control. I did not even want to control it.

He went on teasing the cock with the end of his shoe. The squawks of that bird were enough to annoy anyone.

"*Would* you mind stopping? . . ." said my uncle wrathfully.

Emile Galantie sat down and Marthe did the same. The Captain remained standing. Like an old child who had been scolded. He was breathing fast. He did not know what to do with his hands; he kept thrusting them into his pockets and promptly taking them out again. He searched for his handkerchief, gave it up, then started fumbling for it again. He turned toward me. His gaze was at once beseeching, embarrassed, excited—and full of that great tenderness for André at which I had so often taken umbrage. I went out of the room, slamming the door behind me.

All my days now are splashed with the colors of that cock; russet, red, gray, and gold. That splash of color lights up my loneliness. For Aline and I are not seeing each other any more. We carefully avoid each other. I told her about

184

my conversation with my uncle and she dreads his freezing sarcasm even more than I do. She has not appeared again in this house. And, for my part, I am confined to it. These days I do not want anything to distract me from André.

The splash of four colors grows larger; the gold and crimson spreads in every direction, till it merges with the shadow of oncoming death and becomes like acid spilled on a stone, hissing and eating it away. And then suddenly everything is obliterated; there is only darkness and silence.

I can see that cock again now, very tall, with short, thick spurs. I can see its bare, salient, granulated crop which is rubbed every other day with rum to make it more resistant, so they say. It never crows, invariably keeps its head down, and looks sideways. Its eyes are hard and always so wide-awake that you imagine that, even at night, the lids are afraid to cover those two pits of hot metal. I can see myself again; I can see Bruckner who comes daily to inquire after the champion. "André Joliet's champion, that's going to be famous throughout the country! You just wait and see! Everyone will be talking about little André's unbeatable cock." I can see all of them; I can see everything. Except André. He is there; I speak to him, I am conscious of him in front of me or behind me, but I never succeed in seeing his face. Or if it does at last appear to me, it is André with his eyes closed and those slightly sunken lips on which the kiss of death pressed too heavily . . .

The cock is having a dust-bath. Bruckner is throwing him wasp-grubs which he has in a paper bag and which he has procured, heaven knows how. Apparently they have an irritant effect on the nerves and people give them to watch-dogs too to make them vicious. The misty child stands be-side him. An invisible hand dips into the paper bag in its turn. "Show yourself, I implore you!" I strain my eyes frantically. Can one want anything so desperately? But the most that ever emerges from the fog is a pair of crossed hands—immobile and icy.

At other times it is a child's voice, so distorted that I hardly recognize it. Infinitely far away from me.

"When's he going to fight? He must be practically ready now . . . We've been getting him into condition for three whole weeks!"

Or else:

"He's certainly longing to fight. He must be getting im-patient. Have you looked at his eyes? They look as if he were always dreaming about another cock and wanting to stick his beak in him . . ."

"Be patient! It isn't the right moment yet. First of all, he's got to get used to us . . ."

"Yes, patience, my boy!" says Captain Bruckner. "Don't forget he was born up on the mountain. The air down here on the coast isn't the same: he's got to get used to it . . . It's a serious business, a cock-fight!"

"And where will the battle take place? Here?"

"Don't worry," says Bruckner. "I'm busy working on it. I spend my days scouring the countryside to find an oppo-nent worthy of him. The date's almost fixed. I'm pretty sure that in a few days, let's say a week from Sunday . . ."

186

THE *Isle*

The glowing splash of color and the sounds that rever-
berate from it. A gray old man with eyes like a spaniel who
will go to any lengths for a cock and a child. Another man,
severe and upright and desiccated who mingles with us
from time to time and jeers.

"You may flatter yourself you make an imposing group
in front of this chicken-house. It's a moot point which of
the three of you is more of a kid! Damned if you shouldn't
be photographed!"

We are in that season when nature is all gentleness. The
leaves of the eucalyptus and mango and breadfruit trees—
the frail arms of the paw-paws in their over-ample sleeves,
murmur to each other of the days when God first created
green things. As if not to disturb their meditation, the
cardinals, red as newly-spilled blood, desert the lowlands
for the aloe fields up on the heights and the bul-buls are
silent under their little monkish black hoods.

"Oh, I wish this week would go quickly! I dreamed he
struck once—just once—with his spurs and tore open the
chest of a big gray cock . . . Is he gray, Captain Bruckner,
the one you're putting up against him?"

"He might be," replies Bruckner. "I'm still hesitating
between two propositions."

Emile Galantie: "My dear Bruckner, I'd no idea I was
associating with a fight promoter!"

The old man's laugh spurts up under the mango trees.
But is it not a little less grating than usual? Emile Galantie
seems to have softened. He seems to regard the people
about him, especially this child, with a less critical eye.

187

"Yes, indeed!" (Bruckner smiled) "I never supposed I should set up as an expert on cock-fighting in my declining years. Please God I don't continue this transformation to the point of becoming a butterfly hunter or an herbalist! Collecting herbs, incidentally, would suit my tastes better . . ."

I come and go among the silhouettes of my shadow-theater whose shapes are lit up and slightly distorted by the crimson and gold blaze of the great cock. Marthe Galantie herself has twice deigned to come down as far as the chicken-house. Charlézenn's children spend three quarters of the day standing in front of the wire-netting. Charlézenn affirms—"on my oath, young Massa!"—that when fighting-cocks are killed in battle they immediately resurrect in an egg somewhere, and become another cock just like the original one. It is only the cowards who die . . . Three shadows; five, eight shadows. But the one I seek among all of them is so evanescent! The shadow of a shadow. Sometimes, in a brief shaft of light from the cock, it stands out clearly for a fleeting moment. But death already has its hand on its shoulder. The mother Malleret insisted André needed is claiming him at last.

"It's in three days' time," says Bruckner, excited as a young man. "I warn you, you'll have to keep a stout heart in your little chest. Fights between men are nothing like as ruthless . . . Look, give this to your cock, it's chopped raw liver. I'm assured it has a terrible effect on his character. Ah, now I think of it, he must have a name. Not Chanti-

cleer, that's too common. As common as Petit-Jules or
Petit-Louis among the Creoles. What shall we call him?"

"I don't know."

"Think! It's up to you to christen him since he belongs
to you ..."

A hesitant pause, filled with the soughing of the sea
breeze.

"Perhaps Cyclone? Or Tempest?"

"There now, why not? I vote for Cyclone. That says
plain enough what it means."

I come and go among the shadows on my screen. It is in
the afternoon that I join them. From eight o'clock in the
morning I am in the Office and I only come home for a hurried lunch. And over there in the rue Mahé with my files
and my pen and typewriter I am often very unhappy. I
think of Aline. Shall we ever see each other again with the
same feelings? Out of despair perhaps, or out of mistrust
of my uncle she has gone off to stay for several weeks with
one of her sisters, over at Anse-Jonché. Is she keeping herself for me? I am tense and torn—I can no longer sleep. I
know how much she needs love and excitement. I am afraid
of having lost her completely. It is like a disease with her.
Did we not sleep together the very day after we met? She is
at the mercy of the first overeager look, of the slightest
comforting presence. Especially in the state she is in now.
I no longer even know whether I want to forget her, to live
another life, or to possess her again. Above all, I hope my
uncle will not mention her to me! I can feel his caustic gaze

lingering on me. "Have you any news of Madame Bruckner?" No, if he were to say anything of that kind, I should be quite capable of insulting him. "Is it true that Madame Bruckner is going to prolong her vacation, that her health is not as good as it might be?" Be quiet! That's no business of yours. The caustic gaze is withdrawn. André takes the place of Aline and I am no less tormented. Is not Captain Bruckner supplanting me in his affection as he tried to do once before? I did everything I could to diminish him in the boy's eyes and now he is taking his revenge. It is because of him that André is smiling these days; his smiles are for him, not for me. It is he, Bruckner, who is holding out a hand to him to bring him back to life. While I file papers and examine documents and calculate interest and send out notices of bills falling due.

"Tomorrow is the great day," says Bruckner. "We're going to rub Cyclone for the last time, rub his chest with rum and castor oil and sharpen his spurs with a file. Long live Cyclone! This is only his début. He'll win many other fights and win many more victories, be sure of it! You and your cock will be the lords of the arena and there won't be an amateur of the sport who won't be jealous . . . Tell me, are you pleased?"

"Yes, Captain Bruckner."

"Really happy?"

"Yes, Captain Bruckner. So happy! I adore Cyclone. I had a dog when my father was here. He was called Topsy and I was very fond of him. But I love Cyclone even more."

"Good!"

Bruckner swivels round on his heels. He is like a
drunken man. He smiles and smiles as if he would never
stop smiling. I have to contain myself not to yell foolish
things at him.

"I shall write to my friend Ludovic. He'll be delighted
. . . Have you got the mixture?"

I enter the pen. Bruckner could never do the job properly.
He has the good fortune to be an old man! I am walking
on droppings and raging inwardly. The great cock has remained as wild as he was when he first arrived and I do my
task too hurriedly, so as to finish with this excrement that
sticks to the soles of my shoes and splashes on to the cuffs
of my trousers. Now I get a blow from a wing, now a peck,
now a dig from a spur. The rum thickened with castor oil
makes my fingers greasy. How extraordinarily ill-suited I
am to this kind of caper! . . .

"Are you coming with us, Monsieur Galantie?"

"You're joking! I've no desire to make a spectacle of myself. You've only to look at me! . . . Besides, with all this
tension still in the air, it wouldn't be a good idea for me to
be with you. The blacks in these parts don't exactly idolize
me . . ."

The little shadow is there, over there and nowhere. I
cannot touch it. Even if I did, I should only touch the
cheeks of a dead child.

The blaze of russet, gold, crimson, and gray is suddenly
extinguished.

XX

We made the two and a half mile journey to Camp-des-Makokos in Yacoob's cart. The cock awaited his hour of glory at our feet. He had been put back into his square basket for the occasion and at every jolt he emitted a plaintive squawk which André listened to anxiously, with knitted brows. He was in a hurry to get there. ("How slowly this horse goes!") All the same, every moment he was growing more and more uneasy.

"I should be so unhappy if Cyclone were hurt! For instance, if he got blinded. They say that often happens to fighting-cocks . . . I'd a hundred times rather be hurt instead of him."

"Look here, will you kindly put away any such notion!" scolded Bruckner, whose cheeks were twitching nervously.

"My word, that's inviting bad luck! A fine champion like your Cyclone getting beaten? It's unthinkable! Everyone knows my friend Ludovic's breeding-establishment is the best in the whole countryside and only first-class birds come out of it. Buck up! We're soon going to give everyone a fresh proof of it."

He too (a few days earlier he had brought out his white jersey again) was defending himself against an evident apprehension. He too had a frowning brow and fixed, staring eyes. He noticed that I was observing him and put on a martial air. He slapped his thigh noisily.

"If it isn't a triumph, then . . . then I'll stop calling myself Théodore Bruckner and saying that my sailors loved me like a father and the ocean like a friend!"

André took my hand. He had staked everything on this cock. He could not have put it into words but it was his revenge on loneliness, on Louis Galantie, on life itself. For the very first time, he was rich. For the very first time, he had an object in life that was not hidden in the mists of a dream, this basket he could actually touch and the marvelous cock inside it. Would the day be a happy one to the end? Was not that too much to expect in his case?

"Oh, if only my father were with us! . . ."

I asked what Fernand would have done. He was silent. He was watching the road go past. The cart had left the asphalt now for a dirt-track. To the left, as far as the eye could see, broken stones and aloes; to the right, a little wood whose edge was clothed with yellow cuscuta.

"We're nearly there," Captain Bruckner warned him. "It's the house over there under the two breadfruit trees. Courage, my boy, courage! Don't look so pale! We shall return to Grand-Bourg in triumph, like the generals of old, and I shall have to start chasing through all the villages again to find you challengers . . ."

He turned eagerly toward me, as if seeking confirmation of this prophesied victory on my face. The muscles of his upper cheeks were quivering more than ever. I had the impression he was clenching his teeth. I gave him a sign of encouragement. I was overcome with excitement myself. But I had a presentiment all this was going to end badly.

Some twenty blacks were waiting outside the low house with the corrugated iron roof. It belonged to a bus conductor. He welcomed us, fat and deferent, and sweating in spite of the relative coolness. He made rounded, restrained gestures and spoke very solemnly. He only roused himself to animation to chase away his wife who had appeared in the doorway at the sound of the cart. What was going to happen was only men's business.

"Come in, Captain Bruckner. Come in, Sir, do come in... Well, little white boy, where's this cock?"

André had taken my hand again. There were too many people for him. He had always had a horror of crowds.

"We're ready when you are . . ." said Bruckner.

He proudly brought out his purse.

"I never gamble, either at races or in the lottery. But this is no ordinary day. I bet five rupees on Cyclone . . ."

"Ah, so he's Cyclone?"

Some of the blacks burst out laughing, but were promptly recalled to order by a reproving look from their host. A very old Creole said:

"Not good, that, not good to give an unlucky name to a bird . . ."

He shook his head thoughtfully.

"It's tempting the devil. We suffered enough this last month of April . . ."

"Don't make yourself ill over it, Uncle!" said Captain Bruckner, jovial and nervous.

The old man shrugged his shoulders, spat, and wiped his spittle with his foot. That was to show the devil that he was despised, that he'd better not risk coming here, that none of the persons present were ready to welcome him.

"*My* cock's called Chanticleer IV," said the bus conductor.

"Of course!" retorted Bruckner, smiling.

André smiled too. Now that he had surmounted the fear which the sententious old Creole had inspired in him, he was holding himself very upright, with his chest a little thrown out, like the Captain. No doubt that was the correct attitude for the owner of an invincible cock? My poor little boy! With his hands on his hips and his head thrown back, he placed a foot on the lid of the basket to confirm the fact that this rare, precious creature truly belonged to him.

"*I* bet five rupees too," I said.

That cost me something. Not only was I kept rather short of pocket-money but I was not at all inclined to rash expenses. And what black looks I should get from Emile

Galantie if anyone ever told him I had risked five rupees on a cock! Nevertheless, it was impossible for me not to participate in the event. The bus conductor—his friends called him Télémaque—accepted our stakes calmly. He slipped our two notes into a tin box, added his own in small change —an interminable process!—and the box was at last confided to the octogenarian who had also been appointed umpire of the fight. A basket almost exactly like our own was brought soon afterward and the combatants were introduced to each other. André's red and gold cock aroused murmurs of admiration. His adversary was smaller than he was but stockier, of a uniform blackish-brown color and with an air of infinite melancholy. The umpire made a lengthy inspection of the spurs of both of them to assure himself that they had not been artificially reinforced. No, all was in order.

"Well, let's get going," said someone.

André gave a sudden start. He went white.

"We'll drink to each other first, if you'll allow it," said the bus conductor. "It's the custom; that way we will part good friends—whatever happens . . ."

He placed on the table some spiced cakes, a bottle of rum, and two glasses, one for Bruckner and one for me, and a tumbler of lemonade for André. He and his companions drank from the bottle. Then he offered cigarettes all round.

The great cock was running away, with his crest bloody, one eye half put out and the other as useless. He did not think of returning the blows he received. It was worse than annihilation. He was fleeing, uttering screams as he ran, a grotesque, pitiful sight with all the feathers torn out of his beautiful tail. He ran round and round the arena, while the crowd howled with derision, round and round, round and round, round and round . . . André burst into sobs. Captain Bruckner forced his way into the ring, imploring that the fight should be stopped.

XXI

Barely twenty-four hours after our return from Camp-des-Makokos, André has been put to bed with another bout of raging fever. My uncle himself is worried and that only increases my own uneasiness. I would have preferred to see him indifferent. This fever came on as brutally as a storm. I admit it is partly due to the nervous shock, to the disappointment, but that disappointment cannot be the sole cause of it. We would be criminal to let ourselves be so easily reassured. Am I not already guilty of negligence? I ought to have insisted that the child should be X-rayed and paid out of my own pocket if necessary. I have been as miserly as you, Uncle. Miserly. Perhaps you have some excuses; I have none. Now, tonight, whether it is a case of

tuberculosis or of something else, we must at all costs penetrate the secrets of this little body. We have no right to
waste any more time; we are on the margin, the stone is as
slippery as soap and in the well there is death.

Malleret reappears. His cheery kindliness has deserted
him. I would like to penetrate his mind. Is he not hiding the
truth from us? "I can only repeat what I've already said,
you've got to do something about it. This child is gradually
dying as a twig separated from a tree gradually dries up.
Fever or not, that's not the important thing—one can cope
with fever! It's what's behind it that counts in this case: it's
the will to live that no longer exists—do I make myself
clear enough? It's exactly the same as if you expected to
keep yourself balanced upright on the edge of a precipice
by letting go of all support." Emile Galantie does not deny
what only yesterday he would have described as insanity. Is
he admitting at last that the heart has its place in a human
being? Captain Bruckner is present too. He swallows his
saliva noisily every thirty or forty seconds. He sounds as if
he were drinking. He is inconsolable for the disaster and
bitterly reproaches himself. Probably he no longer has the
courage to undress at night or else he keeps himself perpetually on the alert; his clothes are crumpled. He can do
nothing but mutter:

"The boy must be saved. What can one do? What can I
do?"

"Bring him out of the shadow," replies Malleret roughly.

"What do you mean, Doctor?"

"Get him out of this prison!" (He is blazing with anger.) "Isn't that staring you in the face? Didn't I tell you two months ago that the situation was serious? I suggested a boarding school but you told me to go to the devil. Good Lord! Doesn't anyone realize that this little animal's got to have some kind of nourishment at last? Not only do you keep him on a chain but you keep him perpetually fasting . . ."

"You're being sententious," says my uncle.

He does not intend to let this Dr. Malleret judge him without standing up for himself. He wants to be haughty and imperious. It is no use, his distress is apparent. He goes out of the room. He does not like anyone to see him in this state.

"We'll wait till this fever blows over," Dr. Malleret goes on. "As soon as the boy's a bit better, Richaume will give him an X-ray. I'll bet my bottom dollar there's no question of T.B.! All we've got here is a child *who doesn't want to live,* who has no reason to go on living. Do you think the death of his cock would have given him such a shock if that hadn't been the case?"

My head is like a house in process of demolition. Doors and windows and walls come tumbling down. André must go away, there is no alternative. Six months of my life are being extinguished like the fizzled-out fireworks of the great cock. I had not realized till this evening how much happiness I derived from his presence. At the very moment I was about to lose him! How lonely I am going to be! Even if Aline Bruckner returns to me unchanged, how lonely I shall be!

"What's the use of feeling his forehead every two minutes!" Malleret says to me, curt as a magistrate.

He has put his stethoscope back in his black leather case. He is holding his fountain pen and his prescription pad.

"He'll be on his feet by the end of the week, I promise you. But that's not going to alter the course of this wretched little life unless energetic measures are adopted by Galantie as well as yourself. Good Lord, man, you're faced with a choice! Make up your mind. I'm not saying I wash my hands of it, that wouldn't be true. But I can do no more, my part is finished . . ."

We go out, he and Bruckner and myself. The air is full of a clamor of bells, dinning into my ears: "Your child's going away . . . your child's going away . . . your child's going away . . ." Half-way to the gate, Emile Galantie catches up with us.

"I'll settle with you later on, Malleret, if you don't mind. Alas, I'm afraid we shall have to call you in again . . ."

He has folded his arms as he does at the Office when he is dealing with a particularly tough customer. Is he trying to intimidate Fate? No, it's no good! He slowly uncrosses his arms, takes his left hand in his right hand and makes his long finger-joints crack.

"I'm paying for my mistake. I realize more and more that I ought to have sent him to Madagascar at the same time I packed his father off there. But put yourself in my place:

fancies of that sort come expensive! And besides I was logically in the right to ask myself what he would have gained by following in his father's footsteps. Would his life have been enlarged and enriched by assisting at the drinking-bouts of Monsieur Fernand Joliet?"

He turns round. He knows, he senses that Marthe is watching him from the window of her bedroom. A heavy shadow up there behind the net curtain moves away and vanishes. For a moment he seems relieved.

"Goodbye, Malleret. My kind regards to your wife . . . The fever will have subsided by the end of the week, you say. I shall be delighted if your prophecy proves to be well-founded . . ."

We go back into the house, while Bruckner accompanies the doctor to the little square on the right where he has parked his Overland—our street is in process of being repaired. Marthe has resumed her sentry-duty at the window. A motionless misty shape behind the net curtain. Was she trying to hear what we were saying? Nothing will induce her to question either my uncle or myself. Might one not suppose that she was interested in André's fate? Yet she has proclaimed once and for all that she is indifferent to him. At least she wants to be, or to appear to be.

"That woman!" growls Emile Galantie. "But for her, nothing would have happened . . ."

It was said between his teeth. Immediately, his spleen rises. He would shake his fist at her, if that would not show a weakness, a lack of dignity that would give her a pretext for castigating him later on. He begins to talk very loudly.

"Wherever her shadow falls, you can be sure in advance what you'll find: misery, illness, filth. She's worse than a serpent. A monster made of ice! A calm bog of ordure . . . calm, oh I grant you she's calm! We could all die without her condescending to break her silence . . ."

The heavy shape does not stir. The net curtain keeps her out of the world—out of our world.

XXII

The first incidents of those four dramatic days that were to become known as "The four days of Bedlam" occurred less than forty-eight hours after Malleret's visit.

In *Our Almanacs,* those annals bound in straw-yellow which the Librairie Martial Dauvergne has published faithfully for the past forty years, you can read this entry for the date of June 27, 1928: "The police having arrested in the course of a brawl Mr. Elie Edwards, known as The Avenger, ex-leader of the recently dissolved Progressive Movement, processions of protesters formed in the neighborhood of the station and of the Central Market. Pretext: the presentation of a petition to His Excellency, Sir Clifford Bilsbarrow. Repulsed by the guard outside Government

House which they were trying to surround, the demonstrators went down to the port, brandishing placards inscribed 'Hunger' and 'Strike' and yelling death to the white population and the authorities. A preliminary clash took place at the corner of the rue du Ruisseau and the rue de la Reine. The police were overwhelmed by numbers and forced to fall back, the order to fire having not yet been given. The rioters whose numbers swelled from minute to minute at the summons of the tom-tom began to loot the warehouses of Albion Dock and New Swan Dock and set fire to a small shed belonging to Jackson Brothers Limited. Passers-by were molested and two employees of New Swan were stoned; one of them wounded. The forces of the police, courageously joined by several civilians on their way to work who had been hastily armed, at last opened fire at 10:30 a.m. One person was killed and seven wounded, one of them a woman. In the course of the day, the strike became general. Continuously summoned by the tom-toms which resounded incessantly, blacks and Hindus poured into the town. The police were once again forced to fire in several localities. A message has been despatched to the cruiser *Effingham* which left at the beginning of the week for Colombo, urgently demanding her return."

The same *Almanacs,* June 28: "A false rumor of the murder of Elie Edwards by the police has spread like a train of gunpowder. Acts of violence have been perpetrated almost everywhere in the Colony. Several fires in sugar-cane fields are reported, as well as numerous cases of looting, mainly of provision shops. The total casualties for the day amount to twelve dead and thirty-seven seriously wounded, of whom four are policemen. Sir Clifford has declared a state of emergency and proclaimed martial law. At the same time he is asking the whites, through the channels of the press, to remain in their homes. The cruiser *H.M.S. Effingham* has announced in the course of the night that she is raising steam and will be within sight of the Island on Thursday afternoon. A brigade of volunteers has been formed, commanded by officers of the Third Battalion of the Royal Engineers which is stationed here . . ."

The leaden morning of a leaden day dawned in steady rain that fell with a quiet, rhythmical drumming that meant it would go on long . . .

It was still dark when a first group of strikers had filed under our windows, almost in silence. Then shouts had broken out, quite a long way away, and the muffled sound of a shot which the mountain had gone on echoing for several seconds . . . If I had not slept at all that night, being quite as much worried about André as about the commotions (we had just read about them in the *Gazette*), my uncle had not even gone to bed. Several times I had heard him pacing up and down the dining room. Toward midnight he had gone and awakened Charlézenn to ask him for coffee: afterward he had drunk a small glass of rum.

When I came down, he was waiting for me, standing up,

and holding himself very straight. This sudden flare-up of
rebellion had restored his personality. He was once again
the old fighter whom everyone knew. If André's illness had
somewhat shaken him the day before yesterday, he gave no
sign of it now. I drank my coffee in silence. He had posted
himself in the bay of the central window and was now observing the street, now staring at me.

"You're taking a very long time over your breakfast," he
remarked at last.

"Uncle," I said, putting down my cup (and I had been
hesitating for a good minute), "I'm wondering if it's a
good idea for you to go to the office. The day promises to be
lively . . ."

He walked swiftly toward me.

"What d'you mean?" he snapped, dry as a stick. "Why are
you talking of 'you'? You ought to say 'we.' Not only shall
I be at my desk as on any other day and at the same time as
on any other day but there's no question of your not accompanying me. Life isn't going to stop because a few ruffians
are wandering about Grand-Bourg this morning!"

He added, rather contemptuously: "I'd like to think you
were expressing yourself badly."

Was I afraid? Yes, probably. But I was worried above
all about André. Wasn't it unwise to leave him alone? If
Emile Galantie had realized this perfectly well yesterday,
since he had let me off going to work—though it was a
Tuesday, a particularly heavy day—why would he no
longer admit it today? And, besides, wasn't it dangerous to

207

leave the house in sole charge of Marthe and the servants on a day like this?

"Don't forget that the Governor has urgently asked the whites not to leave their homes," I said. "I'm not remembering it as much for my sake as yours. You're not popular in Grand-Bourg . . ."

"All the more reason for showing these people I despise them . . ."

"Foolhardiness isn't courage," I observed. "Your life is precious to a great many people, if only to your family."

He gave a jeering but nervous laugh. A second rifle shot or revolver shot cracked out, no nearer than the preceding one and with the same long echoing repercussions. I started. Even though he wanted to be a man of marble, Emile Galantie could not repress a shiver. As if to wipe out what he considered unworthy of him, he turned acrid.

"If you really wish to succeed me in the rue Mahé you'd better overcome your cowardice without delay. It is ten to eight. I have never arrived late at the office . . ."

"Oh, it's not my own fate I'm worrying about, you might at least give me credit for that."

"Is it mine? I absolve you from your solicitude."

"It's André, it's the house. Dare we abandon them when anything might happen at any moment?"

"Don't worry," he said with a sour laugh, "your Aunt Marthe would put Satan in person to flight. Have you any doubt of that? Remember the mythical Medusa!"

Nothing would restrain him. The tormented man of yes-

terday had vanished. Maître Galantie was being resurrected
from his catacomb. Summoned by what he considered to be
his first duty? Above all, by pride and also by love of that
white building in the rue Mahé under its myrobalans. Was
that not his spiritual home?

"Does this race of Cain good to realize its bellowings
don't frighten us. If everyone behaved the same way instead of skunking indoors, things would be very different.
Are you ready? Charlézia will keep an eye on André. I suppose, in case of necessity, your aunt might for once be willing to leave her ivory tower? In any case, there's the
telephone."

I followed him, but wishing him in Hades. Here, André
ill, the house defenseless, and over there, not only the safe,
an obvious temptation to reckless men, but Emile Galantie's own person which might provoke violence. He was
really hated by the poor people of Grand-Bourg. What was
going to happen?

The wind, the swaying trees, the wet, cheerless roofs,
the closed shutters in most of the houses, everything was
mysterious and menacing. There are peculiar moments in
life when inanimate things seem to send you a warning
message, a desperate, kindly appeal that you are insane to
ignore. You continue on your way impelled by necessity or
boastfulness or heedlessness, but you are well aware of this
cloud of reproach and of grave warning hovering over you.
You know that you are doing wrong but it is too late to
turn back. And when the irreparable hour strikes you know

—at last—that its sound is what has been ringing in your ears ever since morning . . .

We passed a group of some forty demonstrators, a mingling of Hindus and Creoles, and, on the other pavement, two constables were walking along with slung rifles. An old man who was carrying a sack, no doubt full of pebbles, merely said: "There goes Monsieur Galantie, he doesn't like the poor people." My uncle was holding his umbrella high above his head like a flag. The constables saluted us affably. One of them crossed the street.

"Monsieur Galantie, excuse me for bothering you. But it isn't very wise to be out-of-doors this morning."

"Never mind all that," said my uncle stiffly. "I'm not in the habit of sitting snug at home when times are stormy."

"They're very excited," went on the police officer. "They've got it firmly fixed in their heads that their famous Avenger's been killed and I shall be surprised if there aren't ructions in the course of the day. A great many of them are drunk already. All night there's been nothing but to-ing and fro-ing and secret meetings and they say groups are coming from as far as Mare-Bleue and Landément."

Emile Galantie smiled, with a mixture of condescension and irony, and continued on his way. For a few moments, he thoughtfully contemplated the great key of the Office before inserting it into the lock. What was he thinking of? Was that key an emblem of his power, a solid proof of that will he had exerted every day and which had allowed him to become a man who was feared and envied? A faint redness colored his cheeks. We entered. I had the feeling of defying heaven.

I felt a little easier in my mind when, about ten o'clock, I noticed a policeman patrolling the rue Mahé. No doubt he had been detailed to keep watch on the only shopping-street in Grand-Bourg. The passers-by could have been counted on one's fingers, servants sent out to buy provisions and hurrying home, for all the shops were shut. They moved fast and furtively, hugging the walls, as if alert for danger, a caste apart, crushed by the whites and detested by the blacks who reproached them with having taken on the complacency and selfishness of their masters. I telephoned to the house. Charlézenn answered me, saying all was going well, that everything was peaceful in that part. André? Well, he had woken up, then when he had swallowed his morning pill, he had gone back to sleep again. Charlézia would not let him out of her sight. I could set my mind at rest. He seemed much better and had asked where his cock had been buried.

I made a pretense of working but I could not work. Impossible to concentrate. The world was pitching and tossing. It pitched and tossed even more when my uncle, on his return from the law courts (he had insisted on going there, even though he knew he would find them closed) announced—oh, quite incidentally as he would say—that brawls had been raging all night at Anse-Jonché and there had been casualties.

"Above all, not a word to Bruckner! He would be anxious and I've no precise details to give him . . ."

He was waiting. What would my reaction be? It would have given him satisfaction to see me in a panic. This morning he needed to hurt someone. To prove to himself he was strong. I said nothing. I felt cold. I pictured Aline wounded, violated—perhaps dead. There are times when it must be easy to go mad . . .

Round about half past twelve, Grand-Bourg was thronged with people. The news was spreading like wildfire—information communicated by the police—that the white and mulatto employees of the neighboring sugar refineries had formed themselves into a militia and were forcing their way through to the town, wounding and killing without mercy. As we waited for their arrival which would deliver us, total silence reigned. One reached the point of longing for clashes and screams, for a sign that one was still alive and could still hope, that one was not caught forever in the tentacles of some gigantic octopus. But the silence of a cathedral or of a crypt persisted. My uncle kept constantly mopping his brow as he might have done in the height of summer. The scratching of his pen on the paper was a comfort to me. That little everyday, humdrum noise at moments made the riots seem unreal. But what could he be writing today? Was he not forcing himself to scribble something, no matter what, to convince himself he would survive the storm, to break the unnatural silence of the world? In my mind I was now with André, now with Aline, then I would return to myself. I was more often in the rue Mahé than with them. Immediate, concrete danger reduces you, in spite of yourself, to the state of an animal; the fear of it is too personal a matter for you to think of anyone else. With all my heart I wanted to think only of my sick boy, it seemed to me that would have protected him. I could not manage to do it. I could only mentally walk up and down the rue Mahé. At which end of it would the rioters appear? Were they preparing at this moment to burst into it? Were they talking of setting fire to Emile Galantie's office? Oh, André, André! And over at Anse-Jonché, what had happened to Aline? No one could tell me. The telephone had not yet been installed in this little village huddled in the sand at the mouth of the river.

The storm burst suddenly. Shouts reverberated out of the blue, at once distant and close at hand. There was a crash as if a mountain had fallen. Simultaneously came the sound of shots. I leaped to my feet. All personal anxiety had left me. "My God, André! The house!"

"Keep calm, will you?" cried my uncle.

Taking tiny steps—his knees were betraying him—he went over to the safe, verified the lock, pulled out a chair, and seated himself with his back to the steel door. But even that did not satisfy him. He got up, grabbed his umbrella, then returned to his post. He held the rolled umbrella across his knees, like a rifle.

"Telephone to Charlézenn," he said thickly. "Order him to shut the wooden shutters and bolt all the doors."

I suggested that it would be better for me to go and see to all this myself.

"You will remain at your desk."

"But, Uncle, it's insane to rely on Charlézenn at a moment like this! He's bound to lose his head . . ."

"Insane?" he shouted, clutching his umbrella convulsively. "It's you who are insane! Your place is here in this Office, where your whole future lies. If it were looted and sacked, there'd be nothing left of either of us. You and I would be nobodies. Are you a man and my successor, yes or no? If you're frightened for your skin, get out of my house and my life here and now."

"Calm yourself, I'm not trying for one moment to shirk my obligation to you. I'm only asking myself whether that child doesn't need me, especially at this moment. Whether elementary prudence, elementary charity too, don't demand that I should be with him at this moment . . ."

"And charity doesn't apply to me?" he said bitterly. "Nor prudence either. I'm not worth it! If I'm attacked, I'm to defend my person, my property and my successor, all by myself? Is that what you want? . . . At least your belly might show me some gratitude even if you don't possess such a thing as a heart."

Fear had overwhelmed him. He was no longer the gnarled archangel who, only a few moments ago, had still

214

meant to be indifferent to what was happening. Now he trembled at almost every one of the shots that were following in quick succession and coming nearer.

"Open the window," he commanded.

He was stifling. He walked, slowly and heavily, over to the window. The rain lashed his face. For an instant, he leaned out a little, listening. Then he turned round again. He was blinking, as if dazzled by too bright a light.

"Perhaps you're right," he muttered at last. "Let's go home. My presence here is a positive irritation to these scoundrels. They're blazing with enough hate to want to destroy not only a man, but his work . . ."

As soon as we appeared, a constable came running up, telling us that he would accompany us, that he had been ordered to do so.

"Leave me alone!" exclaimed Emile Galantie. "I'm not an old woman. I forbid you to follow me."

The policeman shrugged his shoulders and followed on our heels. My uncle, though humiliated, was not, at heart, annoyed by his presence. He recovered his lordly air all the more easily now that he knew he was protected and we were getting further and further away from the rioting which seemed to be centered around the neighborhood of the station.

Now I could make out the house, intact and peaceful, and I could quicken my step without being accused of deserting my uncle. The constable had stopped at the crossroads. The noises of the riot only reached us now as distant echoes. I rushed upstairs and flung open André's door. The bed and the room were empty! I uttered a cry of horror. My uncle was at that moment just entering the passage. He threw up his hands and pressed them against his chest.

"Whatever's the matter?"

He came up to me with a tottering step.

"Answer! What's happened?"

"André's disappeared!"

"You're losing your head."

Oh yes, I was losing my head. Ten rifles aiming point-blank at me could not have thrown me into more panic. Where was my boy? Had the shots and the shouting frightened him? Had he taken refuge with Aunt Marthe? That was hardly likely. Suddenly I noticed that his gray overcoat was no longer on the hanger.

"What's Charlézia up to?" exclaimed my uncle, pushing me aside with his arm and entering the bedroom in turn. "What's Charlézia up to? Charlézia, come here at once!"

"I was looking for him," said Charlézia, in tears.

Charlézenn emerged from the kitchen behind her.

"We've been all down the street as far as the little square and all down the rue Mamet too," he said, hanging his head. "Nothing! Madame Marthe herself has searched . . . I wanted to go as far as the police-station, but the road's barred and no one's allowed to . . ."

I had clutched Charlézenn's neck in both hands. I would

have strangled him if my uncle had not intervened. A steam-engine was whistling in my head. There was a mist in front of my eyes.

"Didn't I order you to keep watch over him, Charlézia?" shouted my uncle.

"I did, Sir. Indeed I did, I swear to you."

"You're lying!"

"It's barely an hour ago he was asleep," said Charlézia who had fallen on her knees. "His sheet had slipped; I covered him over again for fear he should catch cold because he was perspiring. And then there were all those bursts of gunshots. I ran out with Charlézenn to get my children in, they were playing in the little square. Everything was quiet when we got back. Madame Marthe asked me for some tea and I made some tea."

"Why of course he's gone out to meet his father," Emile Galantie muttered under his breath. "In his unhinged little mind, wouldn't the revolution mean he was coming back to him?"

He flung himself on me.

"You're the guilty one," he yelled, plowing his nails into my shoulders. "A hundred times I've told you it was criminal to keep up this legend! A hundred times. Now admire your work. Whatever happens, it will be your fault . . . Oh yes, you think that if you'd left the Office in time, we shouldn't be where we are? Well, you owe yourself to the Office, do you hear me? First and foremost to the Office . . ."

I escaped from him. What was impelling me toward

217

the veranda, toward the landing-stage? The noise of the firing, the muffled roar of the crowd no longer reached me. I was walking like an automaton. I saw him. He was right at the end of the little jetty, his feet in the water, Captain Bruckner's telescope pointed toward the horizon. Toward an imaginary ship coming from Madagascar. He was soaked to the skin. I took him by the hand, without a word, and he did not resist. He looked at me without seeing me. He did not see anyone or anything except that dream which had been extinguished forever.

XXIII

I am alone now with my little dead boy. Leave me in peace! It was all over a long time ago. He went between two o'clock and three o'clock. The room smells of wax-polish and of innocence. Is it thirty-two years since it happened or was it today? I have lived every minute of that death agony and my eyelids are leaden with sleep. Take him away if you want to, I am past everything. I should collapse at the faintest breath. No! I can hear you coming in. Go away! Go away! I shall resist. I want to go on watching all alone. Uncle, I don't want your pitying hands on my shoulders, take them off. I hate you. And kindly tell Captain Bruckner not to come in every five minutes and snuffle behind my back.

The riot had stopped at dawn, at the same time the pneumonia declared itself. Doctor Malleret had not been able to get here till nine. His car had been damaged and not a single cart was available, and he had been afraid to venture out on foot in the streets which were still extremely dangerous. "Pneumonia. As sure as two and two make four." He is doomed, isn't he, Doctor? Not the slightest hope? Why don't you answer? For God's sake, answer! Your eyes are a sentence of death. Both lungs are attacked? But say so straight out, why all this shilly-shallying? As if I hadn't seen death enter the room with you! "How could he have been allowed to go out? It was raving madness! It was criminal!" No one *allowed* him to go out, don't incriminate anyone, Doctor. I could willingly have killed Charlézia but I realized it was not her fault. He went out because he had to, that is all; he would have gone out, no matter how, no matter what it cost him because all that shooting and brawling and yelling meant that his father was on the way . . . The boat from Madagascar had suddenly appeared on the horizon, growing larger and larger till it became enormous, luminous, the sun itself.

You diagnosed pneumonia. If he had not caught a chill, death would have taken another shape, but he would have died in any case. You say it was Fernand Joliet who murdered him? It was I. It was each one of us. It was the world and it was God.

All through his delirium, he talked of nothing but Louis Galantie. That gall Louis Galantie had made him drink

—which I thought I had cured him of—had poisoned everything with bitterness. Since the revolution had broken out and his father had not kept his tryst—the tryst he had already failed a few weeks earlier—did not that prove that his hero only really existed in the guise of the drunkard, the forger, the human wreck Louis had denounced to him? Would *you* have gone on living, in his place? Spare me your admonitions, I beg you. You have signed the death certificate, go away. You have children: bring him to life again in the eyes of your children. *I* have no one . . .

Listen to me, André. You cannot answer me. But answer me with your cold body, with your small hands that are so hard, like white roots. Did you love me?

Did you love me?

André! . . .

I have made a home in myself for your spirit, but that spirit is dumb. If only I could teach it to speak to me! If only it were possible to know its secrets, its lights and shadows! What picture did you see in your mind as you died, boy? Did I appear in it? No doubt there was no one but Louis and he kept drawing and drawing and drawing your father for you endlessly, without ever stopping. Unwearyingly he kept painting the miserable truth of that man. He acquired the amplitude of an organ, he reverberated from the very depths of the future and you could not shut your ears to his words. Worse still, you uttered them to yourself: "Your father will never come back." Am I wrong in believing he told you that? "He will never come

221

back as the man you thought you loved, the noble revolutionary with his beautiful, martyr's face. He's a bloated
alcoholic, he's a thief caught with his hand in the till, a
sponger, a swine."

How shriveled your face was, my boy! And your luster-
less eyes, your neck with its swollen veins like the neck
of an old man. *You died old.* The most atrocious thing
they could have inflicted on you. You died a gnarled old
man, disillusioned with everything, betrayed by everything,
scoffed at, smirched—and how could I have struggled
against that transformation? Its roots had been growing
too long and this was the final black fruit it produced. You
were in your last agony and I agonized with you. I asked
you: "Is it true you mistrusted me because of Aline? That
you couldn't believe me any more, that I frightened you,
that, but for that, I might have prevented the tragedy?"
And that riot too, which for you was a blaze of trumpets
heralding the sun, should I have taken part in it, replaced
your father and carried on the dream, made myself a shining figure in your eyes, for your sake? You needed to see
a shining halo, for childhood is something in the dark. A
plaything of God in the dark. But I had not the courage
to be that man. Everything kept me apart from the blacks,
I did not yet love the orphan face of poverty. My uncle
ruled me with a rod of iron as if I were a boy in my teens.
I obeyed. I found the satisfaction of a dog in obeying. I was
by nature deferential and servile where my bread-and-but-
ter was concerned and I had not the temperament of a
fighter.

222

I am close to you. I stroke your forehead as if you could feel me stroking it. Its coldness has a peculiar, almost granulated texture—like the wattles of your game-cock. I love you. How can you ever realize the place you held in my life? You were the living hedge and if it is uprooted, the landscape is bare. You were the bird in the living hedge. The shelter from the sea-wind . . .

Leave me alone, Uncle, I implore you! I order you to! Tell Captain Bruckner to go away too! And make Charlézia stop sobbing in the passage, it's unbearable. For God's sake, go away all of you and leave me in peace.

I am with you. You are nothing now but bones and silence. Ah, God, is death your servant or a sacrilege committed by time to efface your created image in man? Bones and silence, how can that resemble you? Where is your glory? Where is your reflected image and likeness? I have implored you, in vain, a child's blood has flowed in vain . . .

Bones and silence and absence. It is like a refrain in my head. Make some noise, so that it will stop. So that at least it will be muffled. Move some furniture—do anything you like!—live and let me hear you living. Just simply out of pity. I myself am silence: I am going mad.

I must talk so I can hold on till they take him away, talk so I shall not collapse before that. Talk . . .

When we used to walk among the guavas at Chamboron or on the sands at Pointe-Emile when the seaweed was all phosphorescent in the twilight, were you a little comforted? When the cyclones had passed and the whole world smelt of leaves—do you remember? When we used to conjure up fabulous Madagascar with alligators lying like green bronze figures on rivers of metal? . . . Alternately I weep and I reproach myself. My fingers trace the course of that very fine vein that runs the whole length of your neck down to your chest. Did I have a tiny corner in your heart? How can I ever be sure now? Perhaps your father guarded its whole domain too jealously and I was no more than another version of that peddler you knew so well who used to come every Friday on the stroke of six with his junk in a tin-box and would not stop pestering till one had bought something. Was I too insipid, too gray? You needed to be dazzled. All I brought you was a perpetual declining afternoon. Thoughtful for you as a woman while not having her intuition.

Now they are opening that door again! What do they want of me? Will people never stop coming in and out? Is it so hard to leave me alone? For afterward there will be emptiness. Forever emptiness. Do you realize even now what that word means—forever?

"It's time," murmurs my uncle.

"You're lying."

"It's been broad daylight for a long while. You must shave and get dressed. You can't go to the funeral in that state."

He sounds gruff, but he is not far from tears. Marthe remains in the doorway. She is hard and pale. Not a muscle of her quivers.

"You can see he's at the end of his tether," she says.

"What he needs is to take a sedative and sleep. What difference will it make whether he goes to this child's funeral or not?"

I shall not give in but she is right, I have reached my limit. Everything is a confused blur before my eyes, everything is swirling round dizzily. Is Captain Bruckner beside Aunt Marthe with his wife or am I imagining it? At all costs, Aline must not set foot in this room! I do not want her to.

Listen to me, my child. One last time. You are going to go away—will anything survive of you or of me either after then? Let me love you one last time. Tell you that I loved you, that you *were* my child. But I have told you so many, many times! What illusion to think I shall find today the words I have always lacked, words glowing with color, words that are love itself, that will keep you with me always!

"On no account must Madame Bruckner come into this room. Do you hear me? Madame Bruckner must not come in here."

"Now, now," my uncle replies gently. "Madame Bruckner is not in this house. She's come back from Anse-Jonché for the funeral, but she isn't here . . ."

"Don't stay by that bed," says my aunt, who is still in the same place. "The hardest moment has come, you couldn't bear it."

I have got to my feet. I am certainly going to fall. Quite certainly. My legs no longer support me.

"Come with me . . ."

It is my uncle. He puts his arms under both mine.

"You're destroying yourself to no purpose, it's absurd. Whatever you do, it's all over. There was nothing any of us could do. I can testify that, during these six months, you've done everything that was humanly possible for this child, and even more. Nothing is your fault. The one person guilty is Fernand."

"Leave Fernand Joliet in peace!"

A blast of burning heat scorches me all over. My forehead and temples are on fire. Everything I look at is red.

"It's you! . . ."

He has let go of me. He is staggering back toward the door, almost into the very arms of Marthe, whom he hates. He is leaning against her, as if to protect himself from me.

I yell: "It's you! It's you!" It seems to me as if I could go on shouting it till the end of the world.

"It's you!"

But I am the dog who can be reduced to obedience by a frown. I bow my head.

226

XXIV

The narwhal's tusk has been delivered. I smiled when the masons fixed it into its socket, smiled at myself and at my life. Once again, I was expecting an emotion that refused to materialize. All that happened was that my varicose veins reminded me more cruelly than usual of their presence, as if to emphasize the passage of time. For an instant, things over and done with came vividly to life again, but I was watching a film of the past, I was not taking part in it. Everything was that fluctuating, elusive gray that you see on the neck of a guinea-fowl.

On reaching a certain age, one speaks familiarly to death, however much one fears him. I often find myself praying him to take Aline Bruckner before me. Then, it seems to

227

me, I shall recover the real Aline. That old woman in Birmingham who wakes up every morning as I do, is not she. Her age masks her for me. I want to *see* her before I go, and her death is the condition of my finding her again. I do not consider myself a monster for demanding that. What importance can there be for her in those four or five years more on earth that remain to her? For all I know, she has varicose veins like me, the least effort makes her breathless, she has deformed fingers which humiliate her; death would be a happy release. And it would bring *me* back to the days of my prime . . .

Many years ago, I wrote her a long letter which I never sent her. A few months after our rupture. I explained to her why I had given up the idea of marrying her after the death of Captain Bruckner. We had planned to do so. My uncle was dead and I could do as I pleased. We were on the point of getting married. I broke it off on the pretext that she was eight years older than I and that this difference in age might weigh too much later on against our chances of happiness. The real truth was that I would only have got married in order to have children and I did not want to have children by her. She had lived in too close contact with André: I should have at once rediscovered him and rejected him in the eyes of those children. I broke with her to look elsewhere. For more than a year, I was engaged. But let me stop stirring up the waters of the Deluge! My engagement was another piece of falsity. I

have loved no woman but Aline Bruckner and I have had
no child but my dead child.

I must definitely write to her one day soon; I want her
to know the truth about me. But is there room in her mind
for such distant reminiscences? Has she not forgotten? Has
she not forced herself to forget? And besides I feel ap-
pallingly embarrassed at the idea of this confession addressed to a woman of seventy. I should have the feeling
that I was showing a lack of respect for her youth, as well
as for my own. Time has made everything stale. Nevertheless, I shall write to her; and, if she goes before I do, I
shall see her again.

Also, before I die, I must go, if only once, to bow my
head over the tomb where my aunt and my uncle lie buried
side by side. Ironic piece of earth! Never have I gone into
that part of the cemetery. A strange feeling prevents me
from doing so, a kind of chill fear. Perhaps because I was
frightened by the joy my uncle displayed the day he found
himself a widower? by the frenzied thirst for life that had
possessed him from then on? This grave in which two
skeletons insult each other is to me a diabolical place. Louis
Galantie goes there to pray sometimes; Jacques, the new
star of the Galantie family, accompanies him. Louis has
tried several times to make it up with me, ever since I
bought back the house which he had sold after my uncle's
death. I have refused his advances politely by telling him
to cast his mind back but I fear he has not understood. Has
he not increased and multiplied Emile Galantie's fortune,

has he not carried on in his tradition, his spirit? As for himself, he says his conscience is perfectly clear and no doubt he is right. His life, which has run so smoothly, has kept him amazingly young.

A life that has run so smoothly! And mine has been one long inner conflict. I have had to battle constantly against myself, constantly being vanquished by the worst part of me. By the man in rubber-soled shoes . . .

Is it pity or contempt I feel as I examine myself this evening when I have once again taken up my pen to write in my notebook? Never any shoes other than black ones, always bought at the same shop: I had not realized till now that I even buy my shoes as a matter of routine, as I do everything else. That depicts me. What else could a man in those eternal black shoes be but the person who is sitting here now?

There is nothing which my exaggerated, instinctive prudence has not promptly sobered down and as it were, taken the heart out of . . . Free as regards Aline, once I had shaken off the servitude in which my uncle kept me, I was free too as regards the form my loyalty should take. At André's funeral, I had sworn to myself I would be the revolutionary whom he had so desperately awaited. I joined the Progressive Movement, still more or less clandestine at that time, but even there I walked with a muffled step. I never had any brushes with the police. When the fact began to get abroad and most of my rich clients abandoned me, I experienced a bitter satisfaction—mingled nevertheless with too much anxiety for it to resemble a sense of victory. As the months went by I gradually, quite unobtrusively became the blacks' lawyer. The first time those words were hurled at me as an insult, I felt triumphant. I thought I could hear André's happy voice ringing in my ears . . .

I thought I could hear his voice again—this time agonized—when Fernand Joliet came to the rue Mahé to inform me he was getting married again. He had settled down and had given up drinking. We did not speak of André. I stopped him at the very outset. That name was not to be mentioned between us. We could only confront each other in mutual silence. Fernand Joliet asked me to arrange a mortgage loan for him to buy or to build a house. The sum was quite considerable; he had, as usual, big ideas. I found it for him. Later on, when his first child— a boy—was born and he proved incapable of meeting his commitments, as I had foreseen, I took over his debt. I did not do it out of charity. Perhaps I had the feeling I was buying my little dead boy from him, now that he had replaced him?

Ancient, ancient waters. What do I gain by stirring them up? The Virgin's bird is nesting in the jacaranda and bringing back youth to the world. But not mine to me. It was too brief ever to be resuscitated. It burned up in a flash and I have lived ever since as cold lava. Every now and then, it cracks, but no more. Thus tomorrow it will crack again and perhaps a little wider open than usual. Four of my great-nieces and nephews are coming to visit me for the first time since I reoccupied this house. There will also be the grandchildren of Thérèse Leduc, my ex-fiancée, who might have been mine. Oh, my heart, how can you still go on beating?

A Note about the Author

LOYS MASSON was born in 1915 on the Island of
Mauritius—a British possession in the Indian Ocean,
originally colonized by the French and still possessing
a large French-speaking population. Strangely enough,
this writer, so remarkable for his poetic sensitivity,
first earned his living as a professional athlete. Indeed, it was the money he gained from his successful
career as a boxer and football player that enabled him
to come to Paris to pursue his true vocation—that of
a poet and novelist. The year was 1939, and Masson
was soon forced to curtail his literary activity to serve
first in the Foreign Legion and then in the French
Resistance. Since the war, his fame as a writer has
steadily grown, and he is now considered as one of
the foremost figures on the current French literary
scene. *Advocate of the Isle*, published in France as
Le Notaire des noirs, was awarded the Prix des Deux
Magots in 1961.

March 1963

A Note on the Type

THE TEXT of this book was set in Garamond, a modern rendering of the type first cut in the sixteenth century by Claude Garamond (1510-1561). He was a pupil of Geoffroy Troy and is believed to have based his letters on the Venetian models, although he introduced a number of important differences, and it is to him we owe the letter which we know as Old Style. He gave to his letters a certain elegance and a feeling of movement which won for their creator an immediate reputation and the patronage of the French King, Francis I.

Composed, printed, and bound by
The Haddon Craftsmen, Inc., Scranton, Pa.
Typography and binding design by
VINCENT TORRE